HEY, GOOD LOOKING!

"Patty! Listen to me," Gail urged. "Three little words can make everything right again between you and Kevin."

"You—you mean 'I love you'?"

"No, I mean, 'Kevin, I've quit!' Your job is causing the whole problem. Don't you know about all the teasing Kevin's been getting? He has to defend himself against people thinking his girlfriend is acting like a boy."

"Do you think I'm acting like a boy?"

"No, but I think you've forgotten that you began doing this for Kevin, to buy him a gift. What are you trying to prove?"

Patty stared at her friend. The person sitting on the bed seemed like a stranger to her. Feeling betrayed and confused, Patty rose numbly and walked out the door.

Bantam Sweet Dreams Romances
Ask your bookseller for the books you have missed

Hey, Good Looking!

Jane Polcovar

BANTAM BOOKS

TORONTO · NEW YORK · LONDON · SYDNEY · AUCKLAND

RL 6, IL age 11 and up

HEY, GOOD LOOKING!
A Bantam Book / March 1985

Sweet Dreams and its associated logo are registered trademarks of Bantam Books, Inc. Registered in U.S. Patent and Trademark Office and elsewhere.

Cover photo by Pat Hill.

ISBN 0-553-24383-7

Published simultaneously in the United States and Canada

Bantam Books are published by Bantam Books, Inc. Its trademark, consisting of the words "Bantam Books" and the portrayal of a rooster, is Registered in U.S. Patent and Trademark Office and in other countries. Marca Registrada. Bantam Books, Inc., 666 Fifth Avenue, New York, New York 10103.

PRINTED IN THE UNITED STATES OF AMERICA

O   0 9 8 7 6 5 4 3 2 1

Chapter One

"Hey, Patty, wait up!"

Patty Simmons turned, her shoulder-length blond hair swinging gracefully, and spotted her best friend on the other side of the Woodstock, New York, village square. Gail waved, then dashed through the slow-moving, light traffic and across the square. Patty giggled as Gail jostled a tourist who was focusing his camera carefully on the town hall. "Gail, you've ruined more pictures of this town," she said, laughing. "Someday they're going to put up a sign around here that says, Caution, Gail White Crossing."

"Oh, those tourists," Gail said, brushing

1

a lock of frizzy red hair out of her eyes. "I just try to ignore them. They're all over town and always in the way."

Patty watched as the tourist focused once more on the town hall. He had a beautiful camera, but he obviously wasn't much of a photographer. He didn't look comfortable with his equipment, and he was shooting right into the sun. He'd get an awful picture or none at all, Patty thought. She looked at the ground. "What a waste of a good camera," she said quietly.

"What?" Gail asked. "Oh, I just heard about Kevin's camera getting broken. How did it happen, anyway? He was always so careful."

"He was doing a photo series on mountain flowers that he hoped to exhibit, and he fell climbing up a ravine. Not only did he ruin his camera, but no one will let him forget it.

"Actually, I was thinking of buying Kevin a new one for his birthday. He loved his old one so much."

"I know," Gail said and laughed. "Kevin always had one arm around you and the other clutching that camera."

Patty giggled. "Anyway, I want to get him something special, but I can't find what I want in the camera shop here. They sell mostly Instamatics for the tourists."

"Hey, I've got an idea," Gail said. "I have to go to Kingston today to see my orthodontist, and I have the car. Why don't you come with me, and when I finish getting tortured, we can check out the camera stores at the mall. I think the Fourth of July sales are still going on. Maybe you'll be able to find the perfect camera for Kevin."

But three hours later Patty knew it wasn't just a matter of finding the right camera. "Gosh," she exclaimed, "I had no idea it would cost so much! I mean, I was ready to spend all my savings, but a really good camera costs a hundred and fifty dollars more than I have."

"So you'll get the money," Gail said, steering her friend into the mall ice-cream shop. "Hmm, your birthday isn't coming up, and Christmas is a long way off. Maybe you could borrow from your mom. Here, we'll think about it over an ice cream." Gail pushed the door open and led Patty to two seats at the counter.

"Oh, no—no borrowing. I refuse to go that deep into debt."

"Well, you could buy him a cheaper camera, you know."

"Absolutely not," Patty said firmly.

"Anyway, there was some decent equip-

3

ment in there for a lot less than two hundred and fifty dollars."

"Forget it. I saw the camera I want to get Kevin. I know it's just what he'd choose for himself. Those other cameras just don't measure up."

"So, get him the same one secondhand."

"For a birthday present? Gail, that's really tacky. I want to get something new and beautiful."

"OK," Gail said, "then go rob a bank. That's the only way you're going to come up with that much money. We'll have two hot fudge sundaes," she said to the waitress.

"You know what I've got to do?" Patty said solemnly. "I've got to get a job."

Gail looked at her friend for a moment in amazement. "You are kidding. That would be the biggest mistake you could make," she said, sounding shocked.

"Why?" asked Patty curiously.

"Because," Gail said seriously, "it's the kind of thing that could ruin a girl's entire summer!"

"It won't ruin my summer."

"Your summer? I'm talking about mine! Who's going to go shopping with me and tell me if I look good in the clothes I try on? Who's going to spend hours talking about boys with

4

me? Who's going to help me with my uncontrollable hair when I have a big date?"

"I never help you with your hair."

"So, I'm exaggerating a little, but you know what I mean."

"Well," Patty said, shaking her head, "you don't have to worry much about not having me around. My chances of landing a job are almost nil. I know kids who have been looking since school let out, and they haven't found a thing."

"So how did Kevin get his job at the supermarket?"

"He had that job last year, remember? They just rehired him this year."

"Well, get him to help you. Maybe there's another opening at the Grand Union."

"That's silly," Patty said. "I'm supposed to get Kevin to help me find a job so I can buy him a surprise present?"

"There's a simple way around that," Gail said and giggled. "Lie."

"Gail, you're terrible. You know Kevin and I don't lie to each other about anything."

"Oh, Patty, I don't mean a big lie, just a little one. Because if Kevin doesn't help you get a job at the supermarket, you'll never get a job at all, and *he'll* never get his fancy camera."

"So what do I tell him?"

"Anything, just as long as it doesn't have to do with cameras."

Patty's watch showed five-thirty when Gail dropped her in front of her house. She opened the door just in time to hear her mother on the telephone upstairs say, "I'm sorry, Kevin, but Patty's not here."

"I *am* here!" Patty sang out and ran for the kitchen extension. "Hello?"

"Hi, gorgeous. I'm calling on my microsecond of a break, so I've got to talk fast. How about meeting me later? We'll have a pizza with Billy and Erica and then catch a movie."

"I'm broke," Patty apologized.

"Hey, did I ask you to pay?"

"No, but you're working so hard for your money, Kev."

"Well, I can't save every single penny for college. Especially now that my camera's broken and I don't have to buy film," he said ruefully.

"OK, but I'm going to have to start treating you, too."

"Great, then I'll pick you up at seventhirty. I've got to go. See you later."

"No, wait! Kevin, there's something I want to ask you."

"Well, ask quickly. I don't want the manager to come by and see me taking an extended break."

"Just hang up if you see him coming, even if I'm in the middle of a sentence."

"What's up?"

"I—uh—want to get a job."

"You? Why?"

"Well, there are some family things. You know, Mom's been having a hard time making ends meet since the divorce. Even though Dad sends money, there never seems to be enough. I know it's hard for her to come up with my allowance. And besides, you're not free a lot of the time since you're working—"

"Hey, I think it's a great idea."

"You do?"

"Sure, everybody's got to work sometime."

"There's only one thing, Kev."

"What's that?"

"How do I find a job?"

"It's going to be tough. There aren't any jobs here. They've been turning kids away every day."

"Oh, brother!"

"Here comes my boss. Let me think on it. Love ya! Bye." The phone went dead.

"Great," Patty said out loud. "Now what am I going to do?"

"How about cleaning up your room like you promised," Mrs. Simmons said, coming into the kitchen. She looked at her daughter's unhappy expression. "Then take a long, relaxing bubble bath before your date," she added with a wink.

That was just what Patty did, and she had to admit, she felt a lot better afterward. She slipped on a gauzy cotton dress and some low-heeled sandals. *Maybe I can get a job in a clothing store*, she thought. *I bet I'd be good at that.*

Patty was just finishing brushing her hair when she heard Kevin's "Hello, Mrs. Simmons," downstairs. She stole a final look in her mirror and smiled. She was five feet two inches with wavy blond hair, pale blue eyes, and a slender, curvy figure. She was strong, but at the same time delicate. Tucking her hair behind her ears, she bounded downstairs to meet Kevin.

"You're on time again," she cried in mock annoyance. "How am I supposed to be ready when you're always on time?"

"Sorry," Kevin said, laughing. "I keep making the same mistake."

"It's all right, you're forgiven. I know it's just because you want to spend more time with me." Making sure her mother wasn't around, she leaned over and kissed him.

Patty looked lovingly at her boyfriend. She'd have been happy just staring at him all day long. He was so handsome—curly wheat-colored hair and laughing brown eyes. He was a perfect size for her, too, not too tall, with firm, well-shaped muscles. "Let's go," she said. "The walk to the pizza parlor is one of the best parts of the evening." Hand in hand they left the house.

"You're absolutely right about the walk," Kevin agreed, drawing Patty into the shade of their favorite weeping willow tree. Hidden under its drooping branches, they kissed again, tenderly and passionately.

"I can't believe we've been together six whole months," Patty said as they began walking again.

"Yep, and wonderful months they've been, too."

One half hour and two or three shady tree stops later, Patty and Kevin were pushing open the glass door of Tony's Pizza Palace just across from the village square. It was a hot summer night, and the place was jammed with locals and tourists. Luckily Billy and Erica had already gotten a table.

"Hey, lovebirds, over here," Billy called.

"We've taken the liberty of ordering a large pizza with onions and anchovies. I hope that's OK with you guys."

"It is if *you're* going to eat it all," said Patty. All her friends knew she hated both.

"Don't worry," Erica said, squeezing Patty's hand, "we really got mushrooms and peppers." Patty smiled. She loved these double dates with Erica and Billy. It was nice just to be with her friends and, of course, Kevin. They'd done the same thing for months now, and it was still fun, pizza and a movie.

That particular night, they went to a 3-D horror movie. Nobody was really scared, but they had fun screaming with the crowd and, of course, wildly hugging each other with pretend terror.

But Patty's favorite part of a date with Kevin was always after the friends and crowds had been left behind, when they'd sit hugging on Patty's back porch.

"So, how'd you like the movie?" Kevin asked, drawing Patty close to him and snuggling in the moonlight.

"Oh, I'd give it a C for plot and a B for gross effects," she said.

"I've got something for you." Kevin smiled and handed her a slip of paper he'd taken from his pocket.

"What's this?"

"It's a list of job openings," he whispered. "I didn't want you to be anxious about it all night, so I didn't give it to you right away, but when we got off the phone, I thought of a way you might get a job this summer."

"Kevin, the competition's really tough. There are too many kids scrambling for the few summer jobs that exist in this little town."

"Exactly. But a person might have a better chance if she could somehow get to an interview first, right?"

"Yeah, but how?"

"I remembered that Billy has been helping his dad at the newspaper office. He does proofreading before the final newspaper is run off. Well, I called him up, and he said he'd be glad to write down a list of all the want ads as soon as he sees them. That way, you'll know half a day before the paper hits the street who's advertising for help."

"It sounds great, but—is it fair? I mean—"

"Of course, it's fair! You're not stealing anyone's job. You'll get hired if you're qualified, and you won't if you're not. It's perfectly honest. And it just might get you a job."

"All right. Boy, I'm starting to get excited.

11

Maybe I'll even have a job by the end of the week."

"I'll be rooting for you." Kevin smiled. "Good luck, gorgeous."

Chapter Two

Patty was so excited that Friday night that she hardly slept. She studied the paper as soon as she got into bed and then spent the rest of the night dreaming about what she'd say at the interviews. She was thankful when the sunlight squeezed under her window shade. Even though she was anxious to begin her job search, she lay in bed for several minutes, enjoying the silence. Then she reached for the list and went over the openings one more time.

Sell Dan-Dee products in your home. Earn hundreds of dollars each week. Call . . .

Experienced photographer needed for portrait compositions. Bring portfolio to . . .

Sales position in local jewelry shop. Must be neat and reliable. No experience necessary. Phone . . .

Experienced haircutter for Reis Salon. Apply in person Monday morning . . .

Forget Dan-Dee! she told herself straight off. Her friend Amy had worked for them and had had a disastrous time. Dan-Dee, a poor imitation of Avon, sold the worst junk cosmetics in the world. Amy had given her a blow-by-blow account of all the hassles she'd had with dissatisfied customers. In the end she'd spent more of her own money on long distance phone calls to the company than she ever earned from selling the stuff.

Patty looked at the other possibilities. Well, she wasn't an experienced photographer, nor was she a haircutter. But there was still the "no experience necessary" sales job. That would be perfect. She knew the store, and she'd always liked it. *That ought to be a big plus when I'm selling,* she told herself. *And it's right in town, too. I can walk there.*

Patty looked at the clock on her night table. It was only eight o'clock, much too early for stores to be open. For several moments she lay back watching the minute hand inch its way across the face of the clock. *This is crazy,* she finally told herself. *I'll be a nervous wreck before I get started if I have to wait around for two hours.* Trying to kill a little time, she went into the bathroom and took a long shower. She wasted some more time reading, eating breakfast, and putting on makeup. By then it was nine-thirty.

Hurrying back to her room, she plopped down on the bed and picked up the phone and dialed the jewelry store's number carefully.

"Hello," a man's crisp voice answered, "Marco Jewelers."

"Uh, yes, hello. May I speak with the owner, please?"

"Speaking."

"Oh, er—" She coughed nervously. "My name is Patty Simmons, and I'm calling about your ad for sales help in—"

"For what?" he interrupted. Then, apparently without turning away from the mouthpiece, he bellowed so loudly it made Patty jump.

"*Marge,* didn't you cancel that want ad?"

There was a moment of silence before the man said, "I'm sorry, but we meant to take that ad out. My nephew came in from

California, and he needed work, so naturally, his being family and all—"

"I understand," Patty murmured, trying to sound as if it were no big deal.

"We'll be running the ad again at the end of August, though, so why don't you give us a call then?"

"Thank you very much," she managed. "Goodbye."

Patty stared dully at the dead receiver for a moment. It was hard to believe that after all of her expectations and nervous anticipation, everything was over so fast! *There's always Monday's paper*, she reminded herself half-heartedly. But deep down she knew that in a little town like Woodstock, she couldn't expect a dozen new opportunities to materialize in a day. She'd be lucky if there was even one new ad.

What's the matter with me? she scolded herself. *I can't give up already. Watch out, Woodstock, Patty Simmons is going job hunting in person!*

First, she decided she needed to look spectacular. She rose and went over to her closet door. She picked out a simple cotton dress and pinned her shining blond hair back into a french braid, adding two beautifully carved ivory barrettes to the sides. She tiptoed past her mother's bedroom door and down the stairs. Her mother had been working terribly hard since the divorce four years ago, and Patty always tried to be aware of how much it meant to her to sleep late on the weekends. It was the one luxury her mother allowed herself.

"I love you, Mom," Patty whispered, shutting the outside door quietly behind her. "Wish me luck with my job hunting."

Hours later Patty strolled wearily into the supermarket where Kevin worked. She found him stuffing groceries into brown paper bags at one of the checkout counters. "Hey, Kevin."

"Hi, gorgeous. How's it going?" he asked, without looking away from his work.

"Terrible is putting it mildly."

Kevin turned to her momentarily as he stuffed a big bag in a waiting cart. "Billy's list didn't help?"

"No, but ask him again for Monday, OK? Maybe something new will turn up. Anyway, today I'm sure I made the *Guinness Book of World Records* for being denied employment by the greatest number of people in the shortest amount of time. I must have been in and out of twenty stores in town so far."

Kevin stopped working long enough to give Patty a quick hug. "Hey, don't be so hard on yourself. What you're doing is pretty difficult. You need a strong ego for the job of getting a job."

"I know, but all these turndowns are enough to give a person an inferiority complex."

"Excuse me," said Kevin to the next customer in line, an elderly man with an understanding face. "Can I keep you waiting for just half a minute, please?" Before the man could reply, Kevin stepped away from the counter and drew Patty aside. "Listen, gorgeous, what you've got to remember is that practically every other kid in town is going through or has gone through the same thing. It's not you personally they're rejecting."

"Thanks, Kev. I know it's not me, but after today it sure is good to hear someone say it."

"You OK now?"

"Uh-huh. I'm fine." Patty smiled weakly.

"Good. Now, I'd better get back to the counter before we're *both* unemployed."

With a loving parting glance, Patty turned around and left the store to try her luck once more.

Unfortunately, the afternoon turned out to be as bad as the morning. After several

18

more hours of dealing with sometimes not-so-polite interviewers, Patty headed for home. She was exhausted and still out of work.

All she wanted to do was get into bed with a good book, but she hadn't even slipped off her sandals when Kevin phoned to read her Billy's latest want ad information. As it turned out, they were all repeats of the Saturday's column except for one, which read:

Builder's Assistant, to join established crew currently renovating and restoring old Carew mansion. No experience necessary. Apply in person on site. 135 Sauger Lane.

A dejected sigh escaped Patty's lips. "Well, that's it, I guess," she said to Kevin, adding to herself, *there goes your camera!*

"Now wait!" Kevin exclaimed. "Don't get so depressed. It's still early in the summer."

"For swimming maybe, not for getting a job! It's hopeless."

"Hey, listen, I know how you feel. I probably wouldn't have gotten my job if I hadn't worked there last year. And, you know, it's not exactly interesting or fun. I mean, anything would be more fun than packing groceries . . ." His voice trailed off. "But let's think about your problem," he added quickly. "Sometimes people don't see themselves as certain types, and that prevents them from even *thinking* of many jobs they *could* do."

"Like what?"

"I don't know, maybe that job for Dan-Dee."

"Kevin, don't you remember Amy complaining to us about what that was like?"

"Oh. Was that the same company?"

"Yes. There's got to be something besides that. Can you think of anything, because I can't."

"I hate to say it, but just be patient. Unless—"

"Unless what?" Patty asked.

"Now why didn't I think of it before. What a dimwit I am." Patty was in too much suspense to catch the teasing tone in Kevin's voice. "It's perfect. It's you. It's—"

"What is?" Patty asked, exasperated.

"Your soft voice and mild manner almost made me miss the possibility. But maybe, like Clark Kent, you'll turn out to be a Superwoman. Gorgeous, the perfect job for you is—a builder's assistant!"

For a moment, there was stone silence.

Then Patty burst out, "I don't think that's very funny."

"No?" Kevin went right on teasing. "But you agreed you wanted to stretch yourself. Just think of how your muscles would—"

"Kevin, I really don't appreciate your making fun of me like this."

"Aw, Patty, you're being too serious. I'm just trying to lighten things up."

Patty was quiet for a moment. "When you said that being a builder's assistant was very much me, what did you mean? Do you think I look tough?"

"Are you serious? I was only kidding. You're so feminine you could never do that kind of work. I mean, picture yourself in a hard hat with tools hanging from your waist." Kevin laughed.

"I'm really surprised at you, Kevin. I never knew you were so close-minded."

"Hey, wait a minute! I didn't mean to get you all upset."

"You want to know something? I don't think being a builder's assistant *is* so ridiculous! I *am* pretty handy, you know. I helped my father when he was working on making the basement into a playroom!"

"But you didn't even finish it."

"So what? I was good at what we did do.

And I also put the wallpaper up in this house all by myself while my mother was working. All I needed was for the man in the store to explain how. And I did most of the carpet laying in my room, too. And—"

"Oh, boy! Patty, hold on, will you please? Listen—I'm sure you were great with those simple jobs, but you can't—"

"Can't what?" Patty could tell that Kevin was trying, in his own way, to calm her down and end the quarrel. She certainly didn't want to argue, but she couldn't stop the rising tide of anger that was swelling inside her. It surprised her. Why was she so concerned about an ad she'd passed over herself? She made an effort to calm down, but the best she could do was to say, "Maybe we ought to take a little time to cool off, OK?"

"Hold on! Will you let me get a few words in?"

"Not now," Patty said firmly. "Thanks for telling me about the jobs. I'll call you soon. Bye." Patty hung up before Kevin could say anything more.

Now what? she thought. The image Kevin had conjured up to tease her pushed itself into her brain. She saw herself in coveralls, lifting a two-by-four, ready with a hammer to nail it in place. But it wasn't a funny picture at all. Not one little bit.

I'll bet a job like that pays more than minimum wage, Patty thought. *Where was that job site? One thirty-five Sauger Lane. And the ad said, "No experience necessary,* she reminded herself. *So why shouldn't I qualify? I can work hard. And I need the job!*

They'll laugh you into the ground, a little warning voice cried. *Don't do it. Don't go for it.*

But Patty was too worked up by then to give up without trying. There were no other jobs out there except this one. It would be a good job. She'd learn a lot, certainly more than she would selling jewelry or cheap makeup. Her mind was made up. She'd go first thing Monday morning!

Chapter Three

What am I supposed to wear for a construction job interview? Patty mused as she flipped through her closet early on Monday morning. She had never had any experience with this particular problem before. Should she go for the conservative, neat look and wear the one-piece cotton print dress with matching fabric belt? No, she'd look too delicate. What about her Jordache jeans and denim vest? She decided against that as being too cute for a real builder's job. Growing more frustrated by the minute, Patty fleetingly thought of asking her mother's advice. Nope, she couldn't talk to her about it. She'd try to stop Patty from going at all.

Finally Patty decided she'd better just look the part. She reached for a pair of regular jeans with no designer's name on the back pocket. She chose a plaid, short-sleeved work shirt and pulled her hair neatly away from her face into a ponytail. Sailing out of the room, she took the stairs two at a time.

"Hey, what's the rush, Patty?" her mother called out from the open bathroom door. "Come give me a kiss and let me wish you good luck with your job hunt. I'm impressed that you've decided to do all this on your own."

Patty impatiently rushed back upstairs. "How can I kiss you? You've already got your makeup on," she said. Also Patty didn't want a lipstick kiss on her cheek when she applied for a builder's job.

"Ohhh, get over here. Since when did that ever stop me from kissing my little girl?" She saw Patty's doubtful expression. "OK, how about a hug then?" said Mrs. Simmons, extending her arms.

Smiling, Patty stepped into the embrace.

Now, let's see what you're wearing for the job hunt," Mrs. Simmons said, holding her daughter at arm's length to get a better look at her. "Wait a minute, you're not even wearing good jeans. Honey, don't you know you've got to dress for success? You've got some perfectly lovely things hanging in your closet—"

"Mom, trust me, I know what I'm doing," Patty said, adding a silent, *I think.*

"I'm sorry," Mrs. Simmons apologized. "Sometimes it's easy to forget that there's more than one way to do anything. I'm sure you're doing your best. Now, I'm on my way to the office, so if you wait a few minutes, I'll drive you into town."

"No, it's OK. I'll take my bike," Patty said, gulping down her nervousness.

Ten minutes later Patty coasted down the main street and into Sauger Lane, a one-lane, gravel road. Up ahead, she caught sight of wide bulldozer marks and scattered clods of dirt leading to a muddy driveway. She got off her bike, leaned it against a tree, and started on foot up the pathway to the site.

The huge old building, once the magnificent home of a wealthy family, looked majestic even in its rundown, ramshackle condition. The two-story mansion had been abandoned years before after the tragic death of its last heir. No one had purchased the building, and it had gone to ruin.

Since then the children of Woodstock had taken it over as the town's official creepy place and haunted house. Patty could clearly remember a few times when she and her friends had investigated the old mansion. They'd egged each other on with dares and taunts. They'd half crept and half run, filled with terror, excitement and mischief, all the way up to the old oak staircase and down again. They'd never met the ghost of the last owner, and as they'd gotten older, they'd stopped trying, leaving the house for younger kids.

That had been a long time ago, and now Patty had a dream about the house. Instead of being one of its explorers, she hoped to be one of its restorers. Well, she'd know soon enough if that fantasy would come true.

Patty took a very careful look at the old structure. As a kid it had been easy to let the rundown condition of the house make it seem strange and frightening, but now she saw that it really could be quite beautiful.

As she turned her attention to the activity around her, she saw three men passing large sheets of siding to two more men, who were balancing twenty feet above the ground on a narrow scaffold. She watched for a short time as they maneuvered the heavy siding. After a few minutes they took a short break. Patty started toward them with the idea of asking who was in charge. But the sight of all that intense masculine activity made her suddenly feel out of place, even a little afraid to ask her question. Looking around, she noticed a trailer parked off to one side of the lot. Deciding it must be the office, she headed for it.

The metal steps rattled under her feet as she climbed up to the screen door. Inside, two men were bending over blue-printed architecture plans, which were spread out on a long wooden table.

"Hello," she piped up. Her voice came out a little squeaky, and she immediately felt embarrassed.

The men looked up at her sharply. "Yeah?" the broad-shouldered, sandy-haired one asked with annoyance. He obviously didn't want to be disturbed.

Patty had a momentary impulse to forget the whole thing, ask for directions to town, and get herself out of there as quickly as she could. But the wave of fear lessened slightly, just enough for her to go on. She opened the screen door, stuck her head into the trailer, and began, "Uh—excuse me—"

"Come in or stay out, will you? You're letting the flies in," the sandy-haired man said.

"Oh, sorry," she said and entered clumsily. Standing with her back against the screen, she started again. "I—I saw your ad in the paper for an assistant, and I'm here to apply for the job."

The two men glanced slowly at each other in absolute amazement. It seemed to Patty as though a lifetime had passed before the sandy-haired man spoke. "Come again?" he drawled.

"I—I've come about the job that was listed in the paper for—"

"Yeah, we know what *the ad* was for," the tall, darker-haired man interrupted. "But what are you here for?"

Both men were looking at her very strangely. Suddenly Patty felt as if she'd grown horns or turned purple. Why did these men think what she was doing was so bizarre? With new determination she answered, "Well, I really need a job badly, and your work here sounds interesting. Besides, it's the only thing around."

"I'm sorry, honey," the dark-haired man mumbled, turning away from her, "but the ad calls for a *male* assistant."

"Excuse me," Patty persisted, "but it didn't say anything about male or female in the paper."

"Yeah," the other man replied. "Except this is men's work. If you advertise for a builder, you expect to get a man."

"But if a man could learn it, I could, too. I'd really appreciate it if you'd give me a chance," Patty said, doing a good job of controlling her growing anger and frustration.

"Look," the dark-haired man said, pointing a finger at Patty. "We don't hire girls. Now run along."

By now Patty was angry. They weren't even going to give her a chance. Well, she wasn't giving up that easily. "I think it's against the law to discriminate just because of a person's sex, isn't it? At least, that's what they taught us in civics."

The man with the sandy hair, who seemed to be the boss, began to look a little nervous. Patty hurried on. "And in your ad you said you needed an assistant, a *person*," she stressed, "without experience in building. Well, I *have* done some carpentry. My father

30

and I worked together on many of his projects and—"

"Oh, you and your father! So, who's your father?"

"Sam Simmons."

"The lawyer?"

"Yes."

"I thought he moved to New York City."

He did. We didn't."

The corners of the boss's mouth turned down, and he shot his foreman a worried look.

"And I've put in carpets and wallpaper," Patty continued with determination. "I'm ready, and, with some simple instruction, I'm qualified."

There was a moment's silence after she finished speaking. Then the dark-haired foreman quipped, "OK, so you can do small interior jobs. But," he said, twisting around and grabbing something that looked like two rulers glued perpendicularly to each other, "can you tell me what a framing square is used for?" He waved the thing near her face.

Patty's heart sank as her gaze focused upon the object. Out of the corner of her eye, she saw the boss break into a slow smile. But she kept her head and replied coolly with new conviction, "I don't know how to use that tool. Why don't you show me?"

The boss rolled his eyes in exasperation. "Mike, can you explain to her?"

"Listen, honey," the foreman began with strained patience, "this line of work is not meant for someone like yourself. How many women have you seen working in construction, huh? And there's a reason for it. Do you have any idea how tough you have to be to get a house built or rebuilt?"

"It's a beautiful old place, or it will be when you're finished," Patty interrupted.

"What? Oh, yeah, sure it will. But like I was saying, uh, you've got to carry heavy pieces of wood. You've got to swing a hammer for hours at a time. You see how high up the men have to go? Don't you think you'd be scared to hang off a ladder thirty feet up in the air?"

"No," Patty said with certainty.

"All right, all right," said the boss quickly. "You got working papers?" he asked impatiently.

"I'm over sixteen. I don't need them."

"Well, then," he went on, "are you aware of what it's like to work with a bunch of guys? Do you know what you'd be getting yourself into?

32

Let me tell you," he rushed on, "these boys aren't sweethearts. They cuss from sunup till sundown. Swearing is second nature to these guys. I don't think they could get by a day without it, even if a thousand-dollar bet was riding on it." He paused to watch Patty's reaction, then hurriedly went on. "Now, you don't want to be put through the embarrassment of having to listen to terrible language day in, day out, just to make a couple of bucks, do you?"

Patty took a deep breath. "You're right about that. I don't like to hear cursing at all."

"That's exactly it, that's just what I mean! Now you understand. This isn't for you." He threw a proud and relieved look at the foreman.

"You didn't let me finish. That doesn't mean I can't handle it," she said with a controlled voice. "If that's the way people talk on this job, there's really nothing I can do about it. It'll probably just be one of the few things that I won't choose to learn from them. But I'll be thankful for all the things they have to teach me that I *do* want to learn about—I really would like to work here. If only you'd try me out, I'm sure that you wouldn't be sorry. Just give me a chance and we'll see."

Patty stood facing the two men quietly. She knew they'd run out of excuses not to hire her. She saw the boss glance at his foreman with a mixture of amusement and annoyance. "All right, young lady," he said, stepping around the table and holding out his hand for Patty to shake. "I like your spirit. Report to this office tomorrow morning at nine sharp. The pay is two dollars above the minimum wage. We put in a full day here, so plan on being put to work the minute you get here."

"Thank you, sir. Th-thank you," Patty stuttered, looking as surprised as the foreman. She took the man's hand and shook it enthusiastically. "I'll be here. Nine o'clock on the button. And—you won't regret hiring me, I promise."

"Well, we'll find out about that," he said. "I'm giving you a fair chance—the way I have to according to the law. But if you don't work out, you'll be gone in two days, remember that. Either way, I have a feeling we're both going to learn something about what a girl can and can't do," he said with a smile. "Mike, the foreman here, will be your direct superior. Now get along, and we'll see you tomorrow."

Once outside, Patty nearly jumped for joy.

She'd done it; she'd gotten a job! And not just any old job. She felt as if she had proved something important. But she knew she'd have a lot more proving to do in the next few days.

Chapter Four

Patty could hardly wait to tell Kevin about her job. Pedaling furiously, she darted into the Grand Union parking lot. She dropped her bike outside the store and rushed through the exit door as a woman laden with packages was coming out. She quickly glanced at the six checkout counters for Kevin, but he was nowhere to be seen. She dashed down one aisle, then up another. Suddenly she spotted him up ahead marking prices on cans of green beans.

"Kevin, guess what!" she cried. "Kevin, I got it!"

Kevin looked up, a confused smile on his

face. Patty ran up to him and threw her arms around him.

"Well," he said, chuckling, "from the way you sound, I think I'd like to get it, too, whatever it is. Would you mind backing up a little and telling me exactly what we're so happy about?"

"The *job*, Kevin. I just went for an interview and—I got the job!"

"Hey, no kidding! That's great, Patty. So, tell me, which job is it? Which one did you manage to beat the entire under-twenty population of Woodstock out of?"

"Remember the one you were teasing me about?"

"The one I was teasing you about?" His face clouded slightly.

"Oh, you know, the one you told me about last night when I got so mad."

"Last night?" Kevin repeated, still not making the connection.

"The builder's assistant job!" Patty cried, a little annoyed at having to spell out the obvious.

"The what?"

"Kevin! What's the matter with you today? I've had to repeat myself three times already." She gave her head a quick toss and said carefully, "The construction worker's job."

There was a moment of uncomfortable silence. "I thought that was what I heard you say. But I, uh, wasn't sure," Kevin mumbled.

"Yep, that's what I said," Patty answered, confused at her boyfriend's lack of enthusiasm. Why wasn't he jumping in the aisles with her? "So, what do you think? Isn't it just incredible?"

Kevin stood there in silence, his expression a peculiar mixture of surprise and discomfort. "Yeah, it sure is incredible," he said hollowly.

"Well, aren't you going to ask me all about it? Like how much it pays and how I got it and things like that?" Patty was still excited, but not nearly so bubbly and ecstatic as she had been only moments earlier. Something was very wrong, but she didn't know what.

"Oh, sure. Go ahead. Tell me all about it."

The empty ring of Kevin's words stung Patty, but she plunged ahead, anyway, pretending not to notice. Maybe her own excitement would touch him, and the strange attitude he seemed to have about her new job would disappear. She told him the whole story of her interview, ending her torrent of words with a nervous little laugh.

"Gee, Patty, that's—that's great."

"How come you don't sound like you mean that?"

"I mean it." Kevin looked around self-consciously. "But, you know, I'm supposed to be working here, not talking." He grabbed her hand and gave it a gentle squeeze. "Listen, I'll catch you later, OK?" He turned back to his work.

Patty stood there for a moment, watching Kevin mark prices. Finally she turned in disappointment and left the store. Mounting her bike, she pedaled out of the parking lot and headed down the hill toward home. Why had Kevin reacted that way? She just couldn't figure it out. She'd thought he'd be happy for her. Patty began to realize how difficult her new job was going to be. And the hard work at the construction site would probably be the least of it. The real problem was going to be people's feelings about a girl doing construction work. *My gosh,* she thought, *if Kevin doesn't understand, how can I expect Mom or those guys at the site to?*

Overcome by the heavy thoughts that were weighing upon her, Patty ground to a stop in front of the post office. Her mother would still be at work, so there was nothing to wait for her at home but empty rooms. She needed a friend to talk to right then. Turning her bike in the opposite direction, she started off for Gail's house.

The chimes on Gail's front door brought Mrs. White to the porch. She welcomed Patty in, saying, "Gail's in her room, dear. Have you had lunch yet? I'm just about to fix something, if you'd like to join us."

"No, I'm not very hungry, but thanks, anyway."

Patty walked up the stairs slowly. She could hear Duran Duran blaring from Gail's closed bedroom door. She wondered how her friend would take the news. At first she'd been positive Gail would share her excitement, but after Kevin's cool response, she wasn't sure. She knocked timidly on the door. "Gail, it's me," she called.

"Come on in," Gail said. "Boy, am I glad you stopped by."

At the sight of her friend's smiling face, Patty's enthusiasm returned in a rush. "Guess what?" she said excitedly.

"Uh, you won the lottery."

"No."

"Matt Dillon called you up and begged you for a date."

"Come on, Gail, I'm serious. Guess."

" 'Guess,' she says. Just like that, without

a clue. OK, I'll try again. Umm, your mother got a new job."

"You're getting close."

Gail wrinkled her nose. "I have no idea. Would you please tell me already?"

"I got a job!"

"You did? Hey, that's great news!" Gail jumped up and gave Patty a big hug. "Let's celebrate. I'll buy my newly employed friend a burger. So tell me about it. I want to hear all the details. Don't leave anything out."

Gail called down to her mom to let her know they'd be out for lunch, and then she hunted under the bed for her sandals and gave her hair a few strokes with the brush. Patty told her how she'd gone to apply for the job and of her encounter with the construction boss and his foreman. Finishing her story, she sat back on the bed, grinning. "Isn't it all just too fantastic to believe?"

"It certainly is," Gail said, laughing. "So now why don't you start all over and tell me what *really* happened? Did you actually get a job this morning, or are you making that up, too?"

"What do you mean?" Patty cried.

"Hey! I like that astonished routine. It's almost convincing, Patty." Laughing again, Gail turned back to the mirror to finish her

41

hair. "Stop with the acting, Patty, and tell old gullible Gail what you did this morning. And this time, please, the truth, the whole truth, and nothing but the truth."

"But, I *have* told you the truth, just as it happened. Everything!" Patty fell silent and waited.

Gail slowly swiveled around to face her again, her mouth shaped in a perfect oval. "You mean that you—you're going to be building *buildings*? For real?"

A nervous giggle escaped Patty's lips. "What else does a construction assistant build, sand castles? You know that big old house on Sauger Lane that nobody's lived in for ages? Well, they're fixing it up. That's the one we're working on."

"But, Patty, how can you do something like that? I mean, it isn't safe, is it?" she asked as she flopped into a chair.

"Well, the people I'll be working with think it's safe enough. They do it all the time."

"Yes, but—they're men! You know, big muscles, strong hands. That's hardly your image."

"I'm really not worried about my image, Gail. I think I can do the job. But I'd really like it if you showed a little confidence in me."

"Patty, it's not just a matter of confidence.

You have to have the strength and stamina for that kind of thing."

"Who was the high scorer on our basketball team?"

"That's not the same thing."

There was an undertone of irritation in Gail's voice that bothered Patty. "May I ask you what you're getting so upset about?" she asked calmly.

"Upset? I'm not upset—yes! I *am* upset," Gail sputtered. "Because the thought of your doing construction work is absurd. Until now I considered you to have average, no, above average, sense. If I didn't have so much to say—I'd be speechless!"

"You make it sound so—unnatural! All I'm doing is getting a job that any other person might have who saw the ad."

"Correction! Not any other person, any other guy," Gail said. "Come on, Patty, just how many women do *you* know who are construction workers?"

"I don't know any," Patty answered defensively. "And I'm not trying to be one, either. I don't know the first, well, maybe I know the first but not the second thing about building. But this job didn't ask for a construction worker, only an apprentice. Don't you understand? All they asked for was someone willing to learn and work. I fit that requirement, I need the job, and the pay is good. So what's wrong with me getting the position?"

Gail threw up her arms. "I don't know what to say anymore, but I think it's ridiculous."

"Well," Patty said, jumping to her feet angrily, "it's certainly nice to know that I have a friend who'll back me up when it's really important. First Kevin gets weird, and now you. I can't take this!"

Patty was ready to storm out of the room, but Gail sprang from her chair and grabbed her by the arm. "Listen, I'm sorry," she apologized, "I really am. I was just telling you how it seemed to me. But you're not me. I didn't even realize until you got so upset that I was saying all the wrong things. I think it's definitely—unusual for you to be a builder's assistant. I mean, not many girls would even have thought to apply for it in the first place. But *you* did, and so there must be other girls, too, who might have. And, after all, they *did* hire you. So that shows it's not as crazy a thing as I said it was, right? Who knows? Maybe *I'm* the crazy one!"

Patty began to feel a little better. Some of her anger was leaving her, drained away by Gail's obvious concern.

"Just think," Gail added lightly. "I'll be the first kid on the block to have a best friend construction worker named Patty."

"Ha-ha."

"Come on, Patty, am I forgiven?"

"I guess so." Patty smiled and added, "But don't ever do it again."

"Don't worry, I won't," Gail said, raising her arms in a surrender.

Patty dropped onto the bed, exhausted from all the emotional ups and downs of the day. "You know, I'm pretty worried about my mother's reaction to this job," she confessed. "I mean, if you flipped out and Kevin did, too, what is she going to do? She'll probably lock me in my room for the rest of the summer— just to keep me off the construction site."

"It's definitely going to take a lot of convincing," Gail agreed. "Maybe you should tell her you got a job, but not what you'll be doing."

"Gail, come on, I couldn't do that to Mom. Besides, she's not going to say, 'That's nice, dear, see you in the morning,' when I break the news. She'll want to hear every detail, just the way you did."

"Then all you can do is be straightforward, tell her the truth, and explain why this

45

job means so much to you. Which, by the way, you will have to explain to me some day."

Patty sighed. "Frankly, I'm not quite sure why. But, for some reason, I feel very strongly about the whole thing. Part of it is that I don't like being told I can't do something just because I'm a girl. That's not fair. And another part of me really wants to do this kind of work."

"Well, it's going to take a lot better reason than that to make your mother let you go to the site tomorrow morning. Let's think about it over lunch. Remember, I promised to treat you."

Although Patty enjoyed spending the day with Gail, she kept careful track of the time and made sure to get home before her mother was due back from work. She knew she'd have to win her mother over, and she wasn't quite sure how to do that. She decided a little good behavior might help so she started to prepare dinner for her mom.

But when Mrs. Simmons came in at six-fifteen, she was carrying a bag full of hot Chinese food. "Oh, honey, I didn't realize you were going to cook," she apologized. "I thought the two of us would have a work-free dinner tonight, so I brought takeout."

"It's OK, Mom," Patty said. "This casserole will keep until tomorrow."

"So how did the job hunting go today?" Mrs. Simmons asked casually.

"Actually, very well," Patty said, taking the casserole out of the oven to cool. "In fact, I got a job."

"You did? How wonderful. Tell me all about it. What will you be doing?"

There was *that* question, the one Patty had been dreading. Well, it was now or never. "Mom, I'm going to be a building assistant." Patty closed her eyes and waited for the fireworks.

"Hmm, does that mean construction work?" Mrs. Simmons asked.

"Yes."

"So, is that all you're going to say? Tell me all about it. How did my daughter land such an unusual job?"

"Mom, you mean you're going to let me do it?" Patty asked in amazement.

"Of course. You're almost an adult now, and you're certainly old enough to make some decisions for yourself. I told you this morning I'd leave this job hunting up to you."

"Mom," Patty gasped, "you can't mean it!"

"Patty, do you want me to talk you out of taking this job? Is that why you keep asking me if I'm going to interfere?" Mrs. Simmons started spooning the Chinese food onto two plates.

"Oh, no, I definitely want to take this job. I think it's going to be a great experience. I'm going to learn all kinds of important skills and get paid well for it, too. It'll give me a new sense of independence. And I can finally get a camera for Kevin."

Mrs. Simmons poured hot water into a teapot with two tea bags and set it on the table. "As I said, Patty, I'm happy for you about this job. But don't fool yourself. It's going to be hard work in more ways than one. Don't expect it to be a perfect, completely enjoyable experience."

"Oh, I don't," Patty said, digging into her food.

"But you're talking about it that way. Believe me, Patty, I know how difficult it is to be a woman working in a man's world. I'm the only female executive at my office. Do you want the soy sauce?" she asked.

"Patty," Mrs. Simmons continued, "let me warn you about some things. People can be very jealous of someone who is more success-ful than they are—especially if that other person is a little out of place. Those men at the construction site, do you think they're going to welcome you with open arms?"

"I—I don't know," Patty stammered.

"Well, your best friend and your boyfriend may express doubts. What do you think less-caring people will say? What about friends who aren't so close to you and strangers?"

Patty looked dejectedly at her plate. "Then what do I do, Mom?"

"Nothing. You go about your business, and if people don't like it, that's their problem. But be prepared for hassles."

Patty looked at her mother thoughtfully for a moment. "You know, that's the most sensible thing anyone's said to me all day. Mom, you really are fantastic."

"You are too, honey, and remember, if things get tough for you, I'm always here."

Chapter Five

"It's going to be a hot one today, Billy!" exclaimed the owner of the news shop. The man seated at the counter on the stool to Patty's right merely nodded and continued to munch on his roll and butter.

No one had to inform Patty that it was going to be a scorcher. She had woken up that morning at seven, and it was already unbearably humid then. But broiling as it was, the remnants of a cup of hot tea sat steaming on the counter before her. She hoped it would settle her stomach. *Just great. My first day on the job*, Patty thought, *and I have to be sick before I start*. She hadn't slept much, either.

"Anything else, young lady?" the waitress asked, cleaning the counter with a soapy towel.

"No, thanks." Patty glanced at the clock overhead for the fifth time in ten minutes. It was eight-forty-five. "Yes!" she said, hastily changing her mind. "Another cup of tea, please."

"That'll be your third. Better be careful or you'll float away." The waitress chuckled as she brought a fresh cup of hot water and another tea bag.

"I figure if my insides get hotter than my outsides, I won't notice the heat."

"Oh, you'll notice it today, all right, no matter what you do."

Patty sat nervously playing with the tea bag for the next ten minutes. At five of nine, she jumped up from her seat, paid for her tea, and walked quickly up the road to Sauger Lane.

The powerful engines on the heavy equipment were already in full gear as she turned onto the dirt road and walked up to the office. Pretending not to notice the funny side glances one or two of the men gave her as she passed them, Patty looked around nervously for the foreman. She caught sight of him and waved. To her surprise and relief, Mike actually seemed glad to see her. He approached her and flung his arm gently around her shoulder, walking Patty back over to the house. He wanted to introduce her to the other workers. Patty and Mike walked toward a slim man with a beard, who was cutting two by fours with a power saw.

"This here—" Mike bellowed over the noise. "Shut that damn thing off for a minute." The roar subsided, and Mike went on. "This here is Tom. He's been with the company—oh, how long has it been now?"

"Four terrible long years," the workman replied, grinning mischievously.

"Now, be nice, fella. You don't want to scare off the new assistant, do you?" Without pausing to let Tom recover from his obvious shock, he continued, "This is Patty. She's on the crew from now on. OK," he said, turning to Patty, "I think we've brought enough excitement to Tom's life for one day. Let's go over and say hello to Angelo."

Mike's huge hand grabbed Patty's shoulder and steered her to where a large, curly-haired man was intently driving nails into a floorboard. "Hey, Angelo," Mike interrupted, "meet our new assistant."

The workman didn't look up. "Hi, kid."

"Hi."

Bewildered by the soft, feminine voice, the man turned his head just as his hammer came down. He missed the nail and smashed it straight into his thumb. "You son of a—"

"That's all right. You can swear," Patty said quickly, trying to let him know she didn't want her presence to change any routines or habits.

There was a peal of laughter off to the side, and a good-looking young man strode over. He put out his hand, smiled warmly, and said, "Hi, I'm Steve. Welcome aboard." With a look of real gratitude at seeing a friendly face, Patty took his hand and shook it.

"All right," Mike said, "you can meet the rest of the crew later. Right now, I have a special assignment for you." He brought Patty around to the back of the house and showed her rolls and rolls of foil-wrapped pink and yellow cottony stuff piled against one side of the building. Mike pointed at one of them. "Pick it up."

So he wanted to see if she could lift it, did he? Patty braced herself for its heavy weight, leaned over, and pulled hard on the yellow fiber glass roll. It flew up, smacking her full in the face, and she had to take a few backward steps to keep from falling. In spite of its huge size, the bulky roll was quite light.

The corners of Mike's mouth began to twitch as Patty said lamely, "It sure *looked* heavy." But he went on as if nothing had happened. Patty listened to him carefully, still feeling embarrassed, as he explained that the circular bands unfolded and were used as insulation. The fiber glass had to be stapled between the wooden studs that framed the walls, he told her. *It sounds easy enough to handle*, she thought, regaining some of her confidence.

"Grab a roll and let's get started," Mike said. Patty soon discovered that the pink rolls were much thicker and heavier than the yellow one had been. It took much more of her strength to lift them. Following Mike up two seemingly endless staircases, she scanned the enormous rooms off to either side of her as she went. They were in various stages of construction. The fresh scent of pine and cedar mixed with the sounds of power drills and saws, hammers and voices.

Mike waited at the bottom of a smaller and much steeper stairway. He motioned for Patty to go up ahead of him on the makeshift ladder. At the top Patty halted. She was still a good three feet below the floor level of the room. She peered across the floorboards, the long, narrow, low-ceilinged attic spread out before her.

"You have to lift yourself the rest of the way."

First she hoisted the roll of pink fiberglass insulation onto the floor above. Then stretching a leg up to the floor while holding onto a board above her, Patty managed to pull herself in.

"Ouch!"

"Watch your head. The ceiling's only four feet high. It's what's called a crawl space. Beats me why the owners don't want to change it to a full attic. If it were mine, I sure would." Then almost as an afterthought, he called up to her, "You all right?"

"Yes—I think so."

"OK. Now, you're going to have to lie on your back and hold this stapler above your head." Patty saw Mike's hand pop into the opening waving a shiny metal object. She reached over and took it from him, being careful not to straighten up.

"You'll have to lie on your side to get the right angle when you're ready to stuff the fiber glass into the side wall studs. Any questions?"

How could she know if she had any questions before she tried to do it? It *sounded* clear. "Uh—no. I think I've got it," she answered.

"Good. Well, then, get to work."

"Yes, sir."

"Mike. Call me Mike."

"OK, Mike," she said, "and thanks."

"Yeah! Don't mention it."

When she could no longer hear his footsteps, Patty took a look around her. Except for a two-foot by four-foot opening on either end of the attic, there were no windows at all. Even those little openings were covered with slatted aluminum, which prevented the air from circulating freely into the space where Patty sat.

One eye burned suddenly as a bead of sweat found its way into it. She wiped her forehead and blinked until a tear washed the pain away. It was only then that she became aware of the incredible heat. The temperature had to be well over a hundred degrees up there.

But, this was her first day on the job, and there was work to do, she thought determinedly. Patty made her way over to the two rolls of fiber glass that she and Mike had carried up, and began to unwind one of them. She decided to begin at the highest point of the ceiling. That would put off having to squeeze into the tiny space along the side where the sloping walls met the floor.

It took awhile before she was able to figure out just how to position her body, the insulation, and the stapler to do the job properly. At first the fiber glass kept falling back on her face before she could staple it in place. No matter how quickly she thrust the stapler at the insulation after pushing it between the studs, it wasn't fast enough to keep the scratchy, prickly fiber glass from plopping back to the floor where she knelt or lay. Pieces of it were falling onto her face, making her feel itchy and uncomfortable. Her nose tickled, and she gave an enormous sneeze.

Oh, this is awful. How am I going to get through the day? she thought.

With sudden inspiration, she found a new use for the pretty blue bandanna that was keeping her hair neatly in place. She tied it over her face, thinking she must look like a bandit in a western on her way to rob a train. She gave a little laugh. *I could use my trusty staple gun for the holdup*, she said to herself.

Patty settled once more to her task. Soon she began to feel the temperature rising in the airless cubicle. She worked on, but as the sun crept higher in the morning sky, firing its rays into the roof just above her, the motionless air began to feel stagnant. She had never experienced anything like it before. She remembered the time she had stepped into the steamy kitchen of her uncle's restaurant in New York City after the air conditioning had broken down. He had chased her out, telling her it was over 120 degrees in there. But even that hadn't felt as hot as this attic did.

As the day wore on, the heat kept building. The cotton bandanna stuck to Patty's soaking wet skin. She felt as if she were breathing through a layer of heated sponge. Every so often when she began to get dizzy, Patty pulled the bandanna off and desperately breathed in the dank attic air.

Finally she fell into a kind of daze in which even the pounding and throbbing of her arm seemed to be unconnected to her. She strained to hold the heavy stapler above her and slam it into the foil wrapping of the insulation.

Patty had no idea how long she'd been at work when Angelo popped his head into the attic, acting like a long-lost friend. "How's it going, kid?"

"Fine—fine." She forced a casual tone.

"Great. Hang in there."

As his footsteps trailed off, she thought, *Boy, I'm glad I had my act together. Now, if I*

can just take his advice and hang in until
lunch.

Half an hour later Tom peeked in to ask
her the same question. She managed to gasp
out the same answer, though by now every
part of her body was bathed in sweat. After
twenty minutes went by, a third worker came
up to the attic showing interest and concern
in how she was getting on. *Isn't that nice,*
Patty told herself, surprised. *They're taking
the time to look in on me and see that I'm OK.
What nice guys they are.*

But even with the good will of the rest of
the crew, Patty couldn't keep going much
longer. She closed her eyes and begged herself
to continue. "I must keep going. I must keep
going. I must . . ."

Every cell in her body screamed for a
break, just a five-minute break. Suddenly
Patty knew she couldn't stand it one more second. Crawling on all fours, she reached the
attic opening and thrust her head over the
open stairwell. The rising fresh air rushed to
meet her, and she just sat there breathing.
After a few minutes, Patty began to drag herself back into the attic. But her body refused
to obey. She couldn't bear the thought of
doing any more stapling.

Maybe I can ask Mike if there's some-

thing else I can do, she thought, reasoning that she had been working on the insulation for several hours already. Anybody would need to change to something else at this point, she decided. But her common sense won out. *I'll be admitting that I can't handle it. I'd be telling them that I can't take the work*, she realized.

She glanced back over her shoulder, and with a deep sigh, she pushed herself back along the floor and slowly repositioned herself under the open studs.

Patty pushed herself for another half hour. *I am not a quitter*, she kept telling herself. But when, almost a half hour later, her weary arm slammed the staple gun toward the fiber glass and hit her thumb instead, the pain and frustration became too much for her.

"That's it! I can't take it!" Patty said, nearly bursting into tears. "I *can't* do this anymore. If *this* is what being a builder is all about, I don't see how I could *ever* be one!" The decision to back down was a difficult one to make. Carefully Patty descended the steep ladder, thinking about what she'd say to the foreman.

Reaching the second-floor landing, she stepped slowly around the litter of tools and equipment that lay strewn about. The makeshift flooring was full of holes. It took her several minutes to safely reach the old marble staircase that led to the ground floor.

Just then she noticed for the first time how quiet the house was. As she descended the stairs to the first floor, Patty glanced around, but the entire place was empty. *Strange,* she thought. *Where did everybody go?* Stepping through the rubble of pieces of wood, sawdust, nails, and tools, she headed for the carved oak door that led outside. Passing several window openings as she edged along the wall, Patty could hear laughter and conversation just outside.

The rest of the crew was just under the windows. Slowly it dawned on Patty that all the workers were having their lunches, relaxing in the shade of the overhanging roof. Her heart sank. No one had bothered to call up to her to let her know that everyone else had stopped working.

It was then that she really knew what it was like to be an outsider. They hadn't even been courteous enough to tell her it was lunchtime. She leaned against the wall, completely crushed. *But,* she thought suddenly, *they all seemed so concerned and interested in how I was doing on my first day. Maybe I'm being too touchy.*

She made her way once again toward the door. But as she picked up the conversation filtering in through the open window, she stopped short. Patty leaned against the side of an open window, straining to hear. At first she couldn't believe what the snatches of words seemed to indicate.

"Are you back in?"

"What do you mean *back* in?"

"Well, as of now, you're out. The time you picked for her to quit has been over by two hours now. So do you want back in?"

Patty's face started to burn. She inched closer to the window to catch every word.

"What times are still open?"

"Angelo's got two; John's got three; Steve didn't want a go at it; Tom bet on eleven this morning, and now he's back in for two-thirty. I've taken five," the foreman said. "That covers it if she tells me that she's quitting at knock-off time. So if you go in, it's either three-thirty, four, or four-thirty. What'll it be?"

"Bet's still ten bucks?"

"Yeah."

"Put me down for four. That should give me time to go up and cry along with her around three-thirty. Hedge my bet a little," he added with a chuckle.

"She won't be there by then," John called. "I'm collecting on this one, and I say she'll be gone by three."

"Oh, yeah? Don't be too sure. Anyway, rules say no interference."

"You mean besides sticking her in the incinerator in the first place?"

"Right! No interference besides that."

The cruel laughter echoed in Patty's ears. She had heard it herself, but it took time for it to register on her brain. They had made bets as to which hour of the day she would be quitting! "The rats!" Patty said softly. Then she realized that was why they'd kept checking up on her and asking how she was. It wasn't to be nice, it was to see how close she was coming to quitting. Tears of anger and frustration coursed down her cheeks. They had planned the whole thing, giving her the worst job and making it as awful as possible, just to get her to chuck it all and run home. They'd *deliberately* made it hard on her. And it had worked—almost.

With a quick about-face, she went right back up the stairs, back to the steamy attic, and back to work. She made sure to sing loudly from time to time, too—just for extra measure. And she kept it up until she heard the guys' pickup trucks rolling out the driveway and Mike's gruff voice calling up to her, "Hey, girlie, it's quitting time!"

Chapter Six

When Patty went home that night, she answered her mother's questions with as few words as possible, just enough to convince her that everything was fine. But her mother knew better. Patty picked at her supper and spent half an hour in the bathtub. Then she dragged her body to bed, utterly exhausted, and fell fast asleep at eight o'clock.

She awoke the next morning thinking vaguely that she'd go swimming before realizing that she couldn't, not that day or for the rest of the week. She had a job to go to. A vision of the still-unfinished attic swam before her eyes. Sticking her head out the window, she groaned. Wednesday was going to be even hotter than Tuesday.

"I don't need this, I really don't," she heard herself saying out loud. But her next thought was of Mike's smirking face as he collected on his bet. "That creep is not going to get rich from me!"

Nine o'clock, bright and early, Patty was on the job. "Hi ya, fellas," she called gaily. "What have you got in mind for me today?" She noticed with some satisfaction that a few surprised glances were exchanged.

Mike smiled as he called to her, "Back to the salt mines, Spunky."

"You mean the attic?"

"Yup. Grab yourself a roll and get to it."

"Somehow I thought you'd say that," she told him jauntily, crossing to the shed where the supplies were kept.

As she climbed toward the attic, Patty noticed an extension cord running up the ladder, but paid no attention to it. It was only when she saw the whirring fan and felt the cool breeze blowing down the length of the attic that she realized what the cord was for. Left where they couldn't possibly be missed were a plastic face mask and a pair of gloves.

"For me?" she asked in wonderment, but there was no one around to reply.

Well, they had to be! And suddenly she realized that the men, or at least one of them, had put them there. *Someone* was concerned for her, even wished her well. She was touched by the thought, and it made her feel great! Patty had come to work that morning only to avoid the humiliation of giving up in defeat, but now she threw herself happily into her work.

The mask and gloves really helped, too. They kept the fiber glass from scratching her throat and irritating her hands. The fan didn't make the attic cool, but it kept it bearable. Her back and neck were stiff and sore from the day before, but compared to Tuesday's ordeal, the morning seemed to fly by.

Patty was working quickly with the stapler when Tom's head popped through the attic opening. She turned to find him grinning at her. *Oh, great,* she thought, *now what's he up to?* She braced herself for something unpleasant.

"Mike told me to whistle to you for lunch. Come on down."

What's the catch? she asked herself, but all she said was "Sure, I'll be right down." Patty had packed a lunch, but she'd expected to eat it by herself. She had no idea what kind of reception she'd get from the others.

She found the men outside eating under the shade of the overhanging roof. "How's it going, Spunky?" John asked.

By now, all the men had picked up on the nickname Mike had given her. She kind of liked it. "Fine." Patty smiled and sat down opposite them. She pulled a ham-and-cheese sandwich and a peach from her bag and began to eat.

She listened quietly to the conversation, which was mostly about baseball. The workers, it seemed, had their own team, which after seven games, was still undefeated. "Hey, Spunky," Tom said, "what position do you play?"

A few of the men exchanged grins.

"I think she'd make a great catcher," Steve said before Patty could answer. "Then she could catch the passes all the men make."

Trying to be good-natured about the teasing, Patty laughed along with them. After all, there was nothing malicious about *this* kind of joking.

How far along with the insulation are you?" Mike asked.

"I've got about a third of it left."

"Getting tired of it?"

"I can handle it," Patty said a bit defensively.

"I know you can, Spunky. I was just thinking that Steve could use a hand with the siding on the garage. That'll give you a break from the heat, which you've earned, and get you into something new. You up for it?"

"Sure, it sounds great! Thanks, Mike."

"No problem."

"Hey," Angelo called to Tom with obvious annoyance. "I just remembered that we forgot to stop off this morning and pick up the flonces."

"The flonces?"

"Yeah, you know, the five-eighths-inch flonces for the door hinges."

"And I need them right after lunch, too. Aw, I always forget something. Now I'll have to make a mad run over to the building-supply store." He stuffed his half-eaten sandwich back into his lunch pail.

"I'll go for it," Patty volunteered.

"You will? But what about your lunch?"

"No, I'm finished," she said, jumping up.

"Hey—that's great. I appreciate it."

"Now, what you need are three flonces, five-eighths inch," said Angelo. "Make sure they don't give you some other size, 'cause that's the only thing we can use here. That ought to run about—how much would you say, Mike?"

"About thirty-nine bucks, plus tax. But you just tell them to put it on our bill. And hurry back."

Patty hopped on her bicycle and pedaled into town. Lunchtime was busy over at the building-supply company. A lot of builders and carpenters tended to drop in to pick up items around that time. Ten minutes passed before a clerk was ready for her.

"I need three flonces, please, but they have to be five-eighths of an inch."

The clerk blinked twice. "Three what?"

"Flonces," she repeated.

"Sconces?"

"No, flonces—flonces was what they told me."

"Sconces we got, but I've never heard of flonces. And anyway, sconces don't come in that size."

"Are you sure?"

"Lady, I know my business. You'd better go back and check."

Patty walked out of the store upset. *I don't want to go back and check,* she thought. *I'd better try somewhere else.*

The only other building-supply store was at the other end of town, a good mile and a half away—most of it uphill. As much of a hassle as it was, Patty had no choice but to check it out.

Sweating and panting heavily, she leaped off her bicycle and hurried into the store. "Please—do you have any flonces? Size five-eighths of an inch?"

A customer at the counter stepped aside as the man behind the counter turned to her with a baffled look. "What's that you want?"

"Three flonces, five-eighths of an inch. They don't have them at the other building-supply place."

The clerk gave her a long look. "So they sent you here?"

"No, but I thought maybe you'd have them."

"Honey, I don't have them because they don't exist. Who told you to get them?"

"I'm working with Mr. Danon's construction crew over on Sauger Lane."

The clerk nodded. "Those characters. Honey, do you know what a flonce is? It's a left-handed monkey wrench."

"A left-handed monkey wrench?" she repeated.

"Something that doesn't exist. They're just having some fun with you."

"Oh!" Patty felt ashamed.

"Listen," the man said sympathetically,

sensing her humiliation, "don't let them get to you. They've just never grown up, that's all. Always looking to play a practical joke on anyone they can."

"Yeah, I guess so," Patty said dejectedly, walking out of the store. But she hadn't gone five steps when she had a wonderful idea. She went back inside.

"Excuse me," she said, a mischievous smile spreading over her face, "but do you think you might be able to make me a flonce? I'd hate to go back empty-handed."

The clerk instantly caught on to what Patty meant. "You know, I was thinking the same thing myself as I watched you leave the store. Follow me," he said, returning her grin as he led her into a back storeroom.

The men were just breaking from lunch when Patty pedaled toward them. Leaning her bike carefully against a tree, she walked over to Angelo.

"Here you go. And I want you to know that it wasn't easy finding these flonces. It seems that they're not kept in stock anymore." Angelo stared at the neatly wrapped package Patty held out to him. "I thought you'd be happier than *that* to see that I was able to locate some."

"Oh, yeah, uh, thanks." He threw Tom a bewildered glance as he took the package from Patty. Tom stared back at him blankly. Patty walked over to where Mike stood watching and whipped out a yellow piece of paper from her pants pocket.

"Here's the bill. It came to only thirty-six dollars and change. They were having a sale."

Sure enough, when Mike glanced at the receipt from the Silverton Building Supply, there it was written in bold letters:

3 Flonces   ⅝ inch $36.35

Steve peeked over Angelo's shoulder. "Aren't you going to open it? Maybe they gave her the wrong size."

Angelo pulled out his penknife, cut the string, and ripped the wrapping from the box. It was carefully labeled Flonces—Handle With Care. Inside the box, wrapped neatly in tissue paper, were three broken lines from a motorcycle chain. Each was exactly five-eighths of an inch in length.

"Nope," said Steve. "They look like the right size to me."

"Know what I think?" said Angelo, staring at the contents of the box ruefully. "I think I've been flonced!"

There was one unified roar of laughter.

One of the things Patty wanted to do with her first paycheck, after opening a savings account at the local bank, was to buy herself a few new pairs of jeans for work. The first thing she noticed when she walked into The Outfitter was a stunning turquoise jogging suit. She could easily have talked herself into trying it on, but first, she had to see how much the clothes she needed for work would cost.

Looking unsuccessfully up and down the crowded aisles of the little shop for the jeans, Patty decided to ask the salesgirl for help. She finally spotted her, coming out of a fitting room. She held a bathing suit in her hand, and some T-shirts were slung over her shoulder. She'd obviously been trying them on. Patty recognized the girl from one of her classes at school, although she didn't remember which one. "Hi," Patty said in a friendly tone. "Do you work here?"

"Yeah, I just got the job a few days ago. My dad's best friend owns the place. Not that I *wanted* to work." She cracked her gum noisily as she spoke. "Don't I know you?"

"I think we were in some class together. Did you have Wolver for English lit?"

"No. Maybe it was Parks for Western civ?"

"That's it. Did you like him? I thought he was great."

"Are you talking about body or brains? I don't remember much of what he *said*, but, boy, do I remember those muscles."

"I'm looking for a few pairs of jeans," Patty said politely. "Can you point me in the right direction?"

"Sure, follow me. Over there," she said, waving two fingers, "is where the Calvins are, down a bit are the Jordaches, after that you'll find Dijons, then Vanderbilts, then—"

"No, no, I need regular work jeans."

"Oh?" The girl turned and eyed Patty more critically. "You know," she said, "those are really out of style. I mean, *no one* wears them. We've got a stack of them way in the back for the jocks. But I haven't seen a girl wearing them for—ages." When Patty didn't respond, the girl added, "But, of course, if you want to see them. . . ."

"Yes, thank you. I need them for work. The designer brands don't let you move too well, and the material's kind of thin for heavy—"

"Need them for work?" the girl interrupted. "What do you do, ride in rodeos?"

"No." Patty smiled casually. "I—I'm in construction."

"Ah, now it's all beginning to make sense. You're the one I've been hearing so much about—you work at that construction site just down the road, right? That must be something else. I mean, all those guys and just you to flaunt your stuff. I'll tell you, sweetie, take my advice. Forget the jeans and get a few pairs of sexy shorts. You'll have more dates than you can handle."

"I didn't take the job to try to get dates," Patty tried to explain.

"Oooh, *I* see." The girl smirked.

"No, you don't," Patty answered crisply. "I happen to enjoy my job. And I have a very serious boyfriend."

"Are you kidding? Are you telling me he *lets* you go ahead and hang around with all those guys?" She shook her head in amazement. Then her expression changed suddenly. "Now I understand! He must be looking to get free of you anyway."

"I don't think I want to stand here and listen to this anymore," Patty said angrily. "You don't know what you're talking about. He cares enough for me that he is willing to let me make my own decisions. That's something I'm sure, with your mental abilities, you'll never have to worry about." Patty turned on her heel and started for the door.

"Next time I see your boss," she called over her shoulder, "I'll be certain to let him know how helpful you were with my purchase."

Patty knew that she never would say anything to the owner and that it was a dumb thing to say, but it had come out anyway.

She was still fuming as she found herself heading for the news shop to call Gail. Within twenty minutes they were speeding toward Kingston in Mrs. White's Toyota.

The girls spent a fun afternoon checking out all the stores in the Hudson Valley Mall, and Patty got her jeans without a problem. A few times her imagination ran wild, and she could have sworn she was being pointed out and talked about by the girls she recognized from school. But Gail tried to convince her she was only being paranoid.

Patty was really happy just to spend a few hours with her friend the way they always had before she'd taken the job. That was when she realized how much her life had changed, how much *she* had changed, in the few days she had been working. It seemed as if everyone was treating her differently just because she was working on a construction site. Didn't they see she was still the same old Patty? It was as if her world had been turned topsy-turvy, but when she came out of it, she'd know who her real friends were.

Patty heard the door to Kevin's father's car slam shut in front of her house. She was already saying goodbye to her mother when the doorbell rang. "Hey, gorgeous," he said when she opened the door. Patty found herself staring at him for several seconds. She hadn't seen him since she'd started her job, and just the sight of him was delicious. She watched him run his fingers through his sandy hair. "Ready?" he asked, smiling into her eyes.

"You bet." They walked to the car. Kevin held the door open for her, then went around to the driver's side and slid in. He didn't stop at the wheel, however, but moved close to Patty and gave her a tender kiss.

"Hello," he said softly. "Did you have a good day?"

"Yep. Gail and I spent some time together. I even splurged with my very first paycheck." She glanced down at her new sun dress. "Do you like it?"

"I love it," he said, not taking his eyes

from her face. Patty giggled and leaned over to share another wonderful kiss.

They couldn't have wished for better weather for the Creative Music Studio's Full-Moon Festival. Patty had wanted to go to this event for years, but she'd always missed it before. It always attracted the best bands and the largest crowds. It was held on a few grassy acres of gently rolling hills with plenty of space for everyone to dance or just listen to the music under the stars.

That night the air was warm but not humid, with the sweet scent of a summer evening. The moon was indeed full. And the line-up of performers was impressive, from jazz to rock to reggae. All the makings of a magical night were there as Kevin and Patty spread their blanket in a field of grass under the evening's first twinkling stars.

As the music got underway, the grounds began to be dotted with more people. Patty was glad they had arrived a bit early. They had a great spot right in front of the bandstand. Every once in a while some friends of theirs would come over to share their blanket and chat for a bit. They wandered around the grounds, meeting friends, looking at the stars, and talking together peacefully.

"Let's dance," Kevin said as the band

onstage began to play a slow song. It was a perfect moment as Kevin pulled Patty close to him. But the moment was ruined when another couple bumped rudely into them. Patty turned, preparing to accept politely the other couple's apology. Instead, she found herself staring at an unpleasantly familiar face. It took her a second to recognize the salesgirl from The Outfitter.

"Oh, it's *you*," the salesgirl said. "Did they let you in here without a hard hat?"

Patty whirled back to face Kevin, who was confused at what was happening. All Patty knew was that she wanted to get away from that girl as fast as she could. She was definitely bad news to be around.

"Has your boyfriend been stepping on your toes, or is he a good follower?" the girl asked with a sneer.

As Patty turned away, she gave the girl the nastiest look she could manage. "Leave us alone."

"Don't let that dress fool you," the girl said loudly to everyone nearby. "That's a boy, pretending to be a girl."

"Hey, whatever your problem is," Kevin called out over Patty's shoulder, "take it somewhere else, all right? We *were* having a good time until the wind blew you in this direction."

The girl's date who, up until that time, had seemed embarrassed at his partner's behavior, now spoke up for the first time. "Watch it, buster. Don't talk that way to my lady here."

"Some lady," Kevin said in a mocking tone. "You'd be doing her a favor if you taught her some manners." At that moment, Patty realized that her worst nightmare was about to take place. She was going to get Kevin into a fight. The other boy lunged at Kevin.

"Hey," the horrible girl cried at Patty, "maybe *you'd* like to fight instead of your wimpy boyfriend!"

"Kevin, let's go," Patty said, trying to drag him away.

But by then Kevin's anger had reached a peak, and he lunged back at the boy. Horrified, Patty looked on as the two started swinging. "Stop it. *Stop them!*" she begged the crowd. But no one was listening. They couldn't have stopped the boys, anyway, without getting involved themselves.

It seemed like an eternity to Patty before the festival security team appeared on the scene. Two uniformed guards dragged the boys from each other and, before Patty knew what was happening, loaded them into separate cars and sped off.

Frantically Patty raced around, asking anyone she passed if they knew where the boys were being taken and if she could get a lift to wherever it was. Finally one of the musicians found out where the nearest police station was and drove Patty there.

She had to wait an hour on a hard wooden bench before she got to see Kevin. At last, when he was brought out, Patty nearly cried. His face was swollen, with one eye blackened, and his neck and arms were bruised. She stood up on shaky legs and ran over to him. "Oh, gosh, Kevin. I'm so sorry. What—what can I say?"

"There's nothing to say. It happened, and now I have to pay the consequences."

"Does it hurt very much?" Patty asked, feeling helpless and stupid.

"Not too much. Listen, I've got to go. My folks are furious." Kevin nodded toward his parents, standing grim-faced by the door. "Look, do you think you could get your mom to pick you up? We still have to drive back in my mom's car to pick up Dad's car at the festival grounds. They're so mad, I think it'd be better if I didn't ask them to drop you off."

Patty nodded silently, trying to hold back her tears.

Kevin gave her hand a not-very-reassuring squeeze and turned to leave. "Look," he added, "it wasn't just the girl. I lost my cool because of a lot of stuff that's been happening, things I didn't have a chance to talk with you about—"

"Kevin!" his father's stern voice interrupted. "Let's go. Now!"

"I, I'll talk to you—some other time."

The tears rolled down Patty's cheeks as she watched him leave the station house with his parents marching behind. She didn't know why, but she felt that somehow she was entirely to blame for this mess.

Chapter Seven

Patty pulled her sandwich from the paper bag as she sat, shaded from the glaring midday sun by a spreading maple tree. She recalled some of the things she had been learning in the building trade in the past few weeks. She'd installed Sheetrock, spackled walls, helped put siding on the garage, and many other things. She was learning that many of the tools with fancy names were really easy to use, once she was shown how and given a little time to practice. She'd learned to use a chalk line, a level, and the framing square, which had looked so confusing at her interview.

So it wasn't the work, she decided, that

was making her life so difficult. In fact, that was the only thing making her feel *good*! During the whole two and a half weeks since the fistfight, Patty had seen Kevin for a total of ten minutes—and that was when she'd dropped in on him at the supermarket and managed to drag him off for a quick soda next door. When she had tried several times to reach him at home, his mother was always the one to answer, telling her politely that Kevin wasn't there.

Other than that, Kevin had made only two quick calls to her, but they had both been to cancel dates planned earlier. And although Patty was terribly disappointed, his excuses had seemed reasonable enough. Once he had been sick with a stomach virus, and the other time—come to think of it, Patty suddenly realized, he hadn't really told her why he was breaking their second date. But he'd seemed so miserable about backing out that Patty remembered she'd ended up trying to cheer him up. *Thank goodness,* she told herself, *Gail's coming back from her trip to Cape Cod with her parents this afternoon. I could use a good friend.*

Patty had gotten a postcard from Gail asking her to keep that night open so that they could catch up on all the latest news. That meant Gail had something important she was dying to tell. Ha! What would she say if she knew she didn't have to make a date with Patty, that all of Patty's nights were suddenly empty? She hadn't realized until just then how much she'd missed having Gail around to talk to.

The day dragged along. Patty felt as if she were moving in slow motion until quitting time when she moved into high speed. She pedaled right over to Gail's house as quickly as she could.

"Patty!" Gail cried as she flung open the door. Patty took one look at her friend and gasped in astonishment. "Does that mean you like my hair, or that you don't?" Gail smiled nervously.

"I—it's just that it's such a surprise!"

"You don't. I knew it." Gail frowned. "Well, say something."

Patty studied her friend. The frizzy red hair, always flying in every direction was gone. Instead, Gail's hair lay in curls close to her ears. "It's so—so—short," Patty burst out.

Gail laughed. "Well, I know that. But look, you've been staring at my head for a full minute now. So tell me how you like it."

"I think—" Patty said slowly, "that you look fantastic!"

"Phew, what a relief. As our car got closer and closer to Woodstock, I started having second thoughts. That's why I wanted you here tonight. I couldn't let anyone but you be the first to see it. I can always count on the truth from you."

Patty laughed and followed her friend up to her room. They picked through Gail's records and threw the Talking Heads on the turntable, then settled onto the bed to catch up on gossip.

Although Patty was anxious to talk to Gail about what was on her mind, she knew that her friend's bubbling excitement about her trip came first. It would be better, Patty realized, to wait a little while until a quiet point in their conversation before she opened her heart about what was troubling her.

". . . and then I almost died," Gail was saying, "when I found out that my mother had gone over to the cottage next door, just went right over and knocked on the door to inform our neighbors, whom she had never met, that a teenage girl had moved next door for two weeks, and didn't know anybody—and did their teenage kids want to come over for supper that evening? Mom had spotted them when she was coming back from shopping earlier. Anyway, I almost died of embarrassment when she told me what she had done. So that's how I met Sandy and Marty."

"Well, tell me about them."

"Sandy is just our age, and I got along great with her right away. Marty just graduated from high school and, boy, is he good-looking! I swear, I had a hard time taking my eyes off him. He'll be going to the University of Chicago in the fall. Anyway, I hate to admit it, but after I got to know them, I was really glad that Mom had invited them over that night. It might have taken me a week before I ran into them, or maybe I wouldn't have met them at all. But after that first night, we wound up spending almost all our time together. It was the first year in ages that I really enjoyed myself at the Cape. Sandy introduced me to some friends of hers whose families rent the same houses at the Cape every year. I went out on two really special dates while I was there."

Sounds intriguing, Gail, who's the lucky guy?"

That was all the prodding Gail needed to launch into a thirty-five-minute monologue about her romance among the sand dunes.

"It sounds to me," Patty said at last, "as if you really like this guy."

"Yeah, I guess." Gail smiled blissfully.

"Do you think you'll ever see him again?" Patty asked.

"We agreed to write to each other."

"Aha! So you really do like him. And he liked you, too, or he wouldn't have offered to write to you from college."

"How did you know that *he* suggested that we write to each other?"

"Did he?"

"Yes," Gail said happily. "Yes, yes, yes! But I haven't heard about your two weeks yet," she said. I figure since you showed up here wearing those messed-up old jeans that you're still a builder's assistant."

"Very good, Sherlock."

"How has it been going? Has it gotten any easier doing that kind of work with all those men? Are you saving enough money to get the camera soon? And are you going to quit as soon as you save enough?"

"One question at a time, please." Patty laughed, then her tone became more serious. "It's a funny thing," she confided. "I've saved lots of money, but I've never once thought of quitting until you just mentioned it. I guess it would be the logical thing to do—except that having some extra money in your pocket can become habit-forming. But, I'm really getting more from this job than money, anyway. It sure was hard fitting in at first, but now I finally feel like the crew is accepting me. It's a good feeling, Gail, a wonderful feeling."

"I can see why," her friend said, nodding thoughtfully. She started getting up as her mother called them to dinner.

"No! Oh, Gail, everything is *not* fine, not at all. In fact, something is terribly wrong."

Gail sat back down and turned to look at Patty. "How come you let me go on and on about my vacation if there was something that important going on?"

"I was happy to hear your good news. And, also, it was kind of hard to get a word in edgewise," she said, teasingly.

"Wait a minute," Gail said and went to find out from her mother if they could postpone dinner a little. Her mother said she could keep it warm for fifteen minutes, and Gail promised they'd be down by then. "Now *what* is it?" Gail asked, worried.

Patty took a deep breath and launched into the whole story of the fight and Kevin's distance from her since then. "And," she concluded, "except for a few cancellation phone calls, I haven't seen or heard a word from him. So, what do you think?" Her eyes searched Gail's hopefully. "Is it possible I could be imagining that he's avoiding me, that he simply has been sick and busy?"

"Patty," Gail began, "do you really believe it's only your imagination?"

"I don't know, honestly I don't," Patty answered, close to tears. "And I swear, I don't know what I've done to make Kevin want to avoid me. Unless he blames me for that fight and—" Tears fell slowly from the corners of her eyes. Patty choked back a sob. "I guess I shouldn't have talked back to that rotten girl in the store. It only made things worse. But I didn't want him to fight. I tried to get us away from there, I really tried. Oh, Gail . . ." It was as if a dam had burst, and Patty sobbed long and hard.

"Patty! Listen to me," Gail urged. "There is something you can do, three little words you can say to make things all right again between you and Kevin."

"You—you mean 'I love you'?"

"No, I mean 'Kevin, I've quit!' "

Patty blinked numbly. "What?"

"That's right. You have to quit that job. That's what's causing your whole problem."

"But—" Patty's head was swimming. "But—how could my working cause all—"

"It's not you working! It's *where* you

work. I know you like the job a lot, but Kevin can't handle it."

"Gail, who decided what was OK for a girl to do and what was supposed to be for a guy? I mean, if a guy has the ability to do a job, no one gives him a problem. So if a girl has the ability to do something, why can't she just go ahead and do it?"

"It should work that way, but unfortunately, it doesn't."

"Well, what would *you* do?" Patty asked expectantly.

"If I had the relationship you have, if *I* had a guy that cared that much for me and I cared that much for him, there wouldn't be any question in my mind—I'd quit!"

"But why should I have to make a choice like that?"

"Because of all the teasing Kevin must be getting. Can't you see? He has to defend himself against people thinking his girlfriend is acting like a boy?"

"Do you think I'm acting like a boy?"

"No, but I think you've forgotten that you were doing this for Kevin, so you could buy him a gift. What are you trying to prove anyway, Patty?"

"Prove?" There was a moment's uneasy

silence. "Well, I guess I'm trying to prove that I can do it. What's wrong with that?"

"Nothing, as long as you don't care who you hurt."

Patty sat up stiffly. "You think I go around hurting people and not caring? You think I'm that kind of person?"

"Hey, don't get all angry at me. You asked me for advice, remember?"

"You're sure making me sorry about that."

"Fine, then don't do it again."

Patty stared at her friend. Feeling betrayed and confused, she rose numbly and headed across the room. Pausing at the door, she took a last look at Gail. The person with the short, curly hair sitting on the bed seemed like a stranger to her.

Chapter Eight

"I know you *say* you love your job, Patty, but I'm starting to get a little worried about you."

Patty looked up wide-eyed from her scrambled eggs. "Why this concern all of a sudden, Mom?"

"It's just that you've become so involved with it that you seem to be neglecting your friends. I can't remember how long it's been since I've heard the phone ring for you."

Patty stared at her juice, wishing she would sink into the floor. "I'm fine, Mom. Everything's fine," she mumbled.

"Honey, it's not good to let one aspect of your life overshadow all the others."

What could Patty say? How could she tell

her mother that it wasn't she who was avoiding Kevin and Gail, but the other way around. She'd thought of calling some of her friends, but the combination of being tired from her new job and being depressed over Kevin and Gail made her not want to be with anyone very much.

"Mom, I don't want you to worry. Things have a way of working out. Isn't that what you're always telling me?"

She saw her mother smile. "How can I argue with my own words? My daughter is finally getting old enough to learn how to handle her nosy mother. Don't bother clearing the table," she said as Patty picked up her dirty plate. "I'll do it. Just come here and give me a big kiss." Patty went around to where her mother sat, and planted a warm kiss on her cheek. "Now, go on. And don't let them work you too hard. You're still my little girl, and I worry about you."

That afternoon Patty was sitting alone in a booth of the air-conditioned luncheonette not far from Sauger Lane. Occasionally, just to get away from the summer heat, Patty went to have her lunch there.

"Mind if I join you?"

Patty looked up, and there, hovering over her good-naturedly, stood her friendly coworker, Steve. "Go ahead, please sit down."

He slid into the booth across from her and picked up one of the menus wedged between the ketchup and the sugar containers. "Hmmm, I can't make up my mind. What did you order?"

"The tuna special. It comes with fries and cole slaw."

"Sounds good to me," he said. The waitress approached, and he looked up at her. "I'll have the same thing as my friend, the tuna special."

Patty liked Steve, but she was feeling a bit uncomfortable with him there. He had asked her to go out with him twice before, and each time she had found a way to turn him down without hurting his feelings. She hoped he wouldn't ask again that day over lunch.

But despite her misgivings, the conversation came easily for both of them. Patty started to relax and enjoy the meal and the company. She was picking up on little things about Steve she hadn't noticed before. That he was good-looking she had noticed when she'd first met him. But now she was observing that there was a lovely, caring quality about him. Maybe it was the way he looked right into her eyes when she spoke. It made her feel that she had important things to say. And his laughter was absolutely contagious. When his face lit up and his eyes twinkled, it made her laugh right along with him. Nonetheless, she didn't want him to ask her out again. She wasn't looking for someone to date. She still loved Kevin.

As the conversation continued, Steve told Patty that he had just graduated from high school but had been working for years, after school and during the summers, in construction. He loved the work, he said. It was a way of combining physical and mental labor. You had to use your head to figure out how to make a building stand strong and sturdy, but you had to use your body to pound the nails in.

Patty understood completely what he was saying. She had always been taught to use her mind. Her body was supposed to look attractive and healthy, but not necessarily to be used in any meaningful way. Now, Steve had just put into words what she herself had been feeling. Having her body and mind work together to create something was very special.

Steve looked at his watch. "Hey, we better hurry back, or we'll be late," he said. "I didn't realize the time had flown by so quickly." They jogged to the site and made it just in time.

Being with Steve made Patty aware of just how long it had been since she had talked with someone in a personal way. It made her realize how much she missed Kevin. Later that evening she made yet another attempt to talk to him. But once again, Kevin's mother explained that Patty had just missed him.

"Did he get the other two messages that I called?" Patty questioned politely.

"Yes, dear, he got the other messages."

"Well, would you please tell him that I called again? And that it's *very* important that he get back to me tonight?"

"I'll be sure to tell him, Patty. Goodbye."

Patty glanced at her digital alarm clock as she put the receiver back in its cradle. "Seven-thirty. And today is Thursday," she murmured aloud. She knew Kevin never stayed out late during the work week. She reached for the latest issue of *Seventeen* and waited for his return call.

Four endless hours, a pile of magazines, and one-third of a book later, Patty drifted off into a restless sleep, still waiting in her dreams for the phone call that never came.

The next day Patty surprised herself when she accepted Steve's suggestion that they go swimming on Saturday at Wilson State Park. He was obviously surprised, too, because he stammered "You—you will? Tomorrow? Great. Just write down your address, and I'll pick you up. Would eleven-thirty be good?"

After she had agreed to go, Patty started having second thoughts, but she talked herself out of them. *After all*, she reasoned, *it doesn't mean I want to get serious with him just because we're going swimming one day. I want to have some company and a fun day at the lake.* An afternoon at the lake was different than a nighttime date, anyway. It was more informal, more like just hanging out with a friend. And it had been too long since she had enjoyed an afternoon with someone close to her own age. Movies with her mother were fun, but not the same as going out with another teenager.

She was going swimming with Steve, she decided, and she wasn't going to back down. It was a good thing she had bought a new bathing suit earlier in the summer with Gail. The next day would be the first time she'd be getting it wet.

Steve picked her up at her house in a new silver sports car. "I'm really into cars," he explained as they walked toward the street. "It's one of the advantages of having worked the past few years. I saved up, and this year I got myself what I've always wanted more than anything." He looked with pride at the shiny car parked at the curb. Patty could see he was proud that he had earned it for himself.

"I've been saving up for something special, too," Patty said softly. "But I—I might not get it after all."

"Hey, don't give up yet," he encouraged her. "The summer's only half over. Everything may still work out just the way you want it to." He put his arm lightly around her and smiled into her distant eyes.

Patty felt real concern coming from Steve, and she shook off her dark mood. "You're absolutely right. Who knows what tomorrow will bring?"

Patty had a great time with Steve on the ride out. They sang along with the car radio and told all the jokes they knew. Finally Steve pulled into the parking lot. Patty carried a picnic basket down to the water and Steve grabbed a blanket from the backseat. They found an uncrowded stretch of sand and spread the blanket out.

"You know, I just realized that I've never seen you in anything but your jeans and a work shirt," Steve said, plopping down alongside Patty.

"Well, this is me as a normal girl," she said and laughed.

Patty and Steve lay soaking up the sun's heat. "Let's go in the water," Steve suggested after a while.

"Good idea. I'm beginning to broil." She followed Steve down to the lake, and they dived in together. The water was cool and refreshing. "Let's swim to the raft," Patty called.

She started a strong, graceful crawl stroke across the lake and swam once around the raft. "I'll race you to shore," she said to Steve.

"Ready, set, go," Steve cried.

He won, but only by a hair. "Hey, don't you know I'm a sore loser," she said as she splashed some water at him. She ran out of the water, laughing, with Steve right behind her—and stopped dead in her tracks, the smile frozen on her face. Not twenty feet away, gazing off in another direction was Kevin! He was standing next to a very pretty girl with long, raven-black hair, his arms cradling a couple of towels while she spread the blanket out for the two of them.

Patty had stopped so suddenly that Steve nearly bumped into her. "Everything OK?" he asked, first looking at Patty's face, then following her gaze to Kevin.

Patty barely heard him. She was riveted to that spot while her mind raced through painful memories. She thought of how she had been phoning Kevin, waiting for him to return her calls. And she had been dumb enough to believe all those stories he had told her when all the while he was probably going on all kinds of dates with other girls.

So he *had* been avoiding her all along. How could he have been so cruel? How could she have been so gullible? Her throat became dry. She just had to get away before Kevin turned and saw her standing there like a fool. Her eyes scanned the flat beach. Where could she run to, where could she hide?

Suddenly the whirl of thoughts whipping through her mind changed direction. No, she wasn't going to humiliate herself any further by trying to disappear. She hadn't done anything wrong. It wasn't she who had lied. Kevin was not going to ruin the first day she'd enjoyed in a long time.

With all the courage and will power she

could gather, Patty turned toward Steve, who was still waiting for some cue from her as to what to do next. "I've had, um, a bit of a surprise, but I'm fine now. So where's our blanket? Oh," she said, pointing shakily, "it's over there."

Steve grabbed her arm as she started walking. "We don't have to stay. We got a nice swim in. If you'd rather, we could leave." He glanced back to where Kevin and his black-haired companion were sharing a sandwich.

"No," Patty said softly. "Let's not let anything spoil any more of this day, OK?" Her eyes pleaded with Steve to understand why she *needed* to stay and to give her strength to do it her own way.

"I'll do whatever you say. Do you want me to bop him or ignore him?" Steve asked, smiling.

"Ignore him," Patty urged.

"You got it. Last one to the basket has to eat leftovers for lunch," he called, and they were off in a flash, kicking sand behind them as they raced to their blanket.

Patty succeeded in pushing thoughts of Kevin, sitting with that girl right on the very same beach as she was, out of her mind for parts of the afternoon. She just pretended he wasn't there. She was careful not to look in his direction, and she hoped he wouldn't catch sight of her.

But at other times she was sure Kevin was watching her—especially when she and Steve stood by the shore, wading into the water. Her back burned with the feeling of his gaze boring into her. But she dared not turn to see if he really was staring, although she desperately wanted to.

Patty wondered if he was jealous. She hoped so. But at the same time, she wanted nothing more than for him to appear suddenly by her side, smiling, and assure her that everything was all right between them. He would give her a perfectly logical explanation as to who that girl was and why he was with her. "She's a visiting cousin," he would say, "who's just come in from Michigan, and my mother told me to show her a good time."

Throughout the rest of the afternoon, Patty felt Kevin's presence on the beach and waited for him to approach her. But he never did.

Chapter Nine

It would have been obvious to a perfect stranger watching Patty drag herself absent-mindedly from one activity to another that Sunday that something was very wrong. So it was only a matter of time before Mrs. Simmons knocked on her door. She felt it was time to have a talk.

But Patty was in no mood for that, either. She tried to explain that, yes, something was bothering her, and, when she felt ready to discuss it, she would. She just needed to think things over.

Patty, usually not one for brooding, felt miserable that whole day. She picked out Kevin's favorite album from her small collection and let it play over and over, all the while thinking of some of the wonderful times they had shared. But her mind kept flashing back to the image of him with that girl at the lake. She imagined how they might have spent the day together, laughing and getting to know each other better. She saw him put his arm around her, just the way he always did with Patty. She even imagined Kevin mocking her to his new girlfriend, revealing secrets that only Kevin had been entrusted to hear, and the two of them laughing together over them.

Finally Patty let tears run down her cheeks, and she understood why she was making herself think those thoughts. It felt good to cry, to let out some of the pain and hurt. She felt better when she finished, but she still had no idea what to do about the situation.

The next day passed in that dull haze, with Patty not being able to concentrate on much of anything. John heard her cry out for the third time as she brought the hammer down on her thumb. He started teasing her about her sudden clumsiness. Steve, realizing that it was not the time to joke with her, carefully steered the other guys away from their annoying game. She secretly thanked him for it.

Sometime later in the day, as her mind wandered over and over what had happened with Kevin, Patty realized what she had to do. It wouldn't be easy, but it was the only thing that made sense, the only way to get a straight answer from Kevin. At quitting time Patty went into the washroom, scrubbed her face and hands, and fixed her hair, trying to compensate for her shapeless work clothes.

Less than half an hour later, she was standing on Kevin's doorstep, her shaky hand ringing the bell.

"Well, hello," Kevin's father said, clearly surprised to see her. "What can I do for you?"

"I've come to see Kevin."

"Did you two have a date?" Patty could tell he knew they didn't.

"No, but it seems I'm not able to reach him any longer by phone. That's why I'm here."

"Oh, I see," he replied. "I'll check his room. Please come in."

Several minutes later, Kevin hesitantly entered the living room, where Patty sat waiting uncomfortably.

"Hi," he said with a tiny, almost frightened smile. His eyes seemed happy to see her, but his face and the way he shifted from one foot to the other showed how nervous he was.

"Hi," she repeated. *Now what?* she wondered.

"Would you like a Coke?"

She accepted, thankful for the few seconds alone while he went into the kitchen. But he returned too soon for her to figure out how to go on. This was turning out to be much harder than she had counted on. Maybe it wasn't such a great idea after all. But how could she get out of it now? She sat there with the glass of soda in her hand, facing Kevin. There was no turning back.

"Kevin," she said, taking a deep breath, "at first when you didn't call or, rather, called to tell me why you had to cancel two of our dates, I believed your reasons for breaking them—"

"Do you mean that you don't believe them now?" Kevin sat up stiffly.

"No, I'm not saying that. I've never thought you were a liar, and I'm not saying you weren't sick when you said you were. But you've made it pretty clear that something is definitely the matter between us. And, I swear, I don't know what it is."

Kevin looked down and flicked some imaginary lint from his jeans. "What makes you so sure something's the matter? It could just be that lots of things have come up."

"You've said you've never lied to me. Are you going to start now?"

A look of hurt swept over his face. "No," he said, "I won't start now."

"I called you. You never called me back. Do you know how that made me feel?"

"I didn't mean to hurt you. You've got to believe that."

"I do, but I've got to know what's happened that's made you not want to be with me." She could feel the tears welling up, and she dug her nails into her hand to keep them from falling. She didn't want sympathy; she wanted honesty.

"I—I've been turning myself inside out trying to answer that question myself, Patty. There was something in me that needed to be alone and sort out some of my feelings."

"About me?" she asked, almost in a whisper.

"No, about things that have happened to me."

"What things?" The image of the black-haired girl flooded her mind. "Is it that other girl?" Patty blurted out.

"What other girl?"

"That must be it," Patty said.

"Of course it's not. No one else could stop me from seeing you," Kevin said gently.

"But I saw you with her at the lake. She had long black hair and—"

"And the guy you were with had blond hair and muscles. I get your act now, Patty. Before, you didn't care how rotten I was feeling. But now that you're jealous, you come beating on my door to find out what's the matter."

"How can you say that? It's me, Patty, remember? I cared how you were feeling, that's why I kept trying to call you. Only you told everyone to tell me you weren't home."

"I wasn't home!"

"But you never called me back," she cried.

"No, you're right. I never did. I guess I didn't want to admit it to myself, but now that you've cornered me, I'll have to come out with it. I can't take it, Patty. I just can't take your working at that job. I know I encouraged you. I tried to be supportive, I really did. But if you knew what I've been going through . . ."

"You mean the fight. I felt terrible about that, and I wanted to apologize for it so many times. Kevin, I tried to get us away from these people."

"It's not the fight. Don't you see? I've had to put up with all kinds of flack standing there packing ladies' groceries while my girlfriend saws lumber. Patty, you can't begin to know what the kids have made of that. I just can't deal with it. If you want me, you're going to have to quit that job. It's as simple as that."

"But—" Patty knew the horrible teasing she had had to put up with, but she never realized how much abuse Kevin must have been taking. "Why didn't you at least tell me what was going on? I guess I should have figured that people might be giving you a hard time—I know what *I* was having to put up with. But it never hit me that they'd be so hard on you, too."

"I didn't tell you because I didn't want to make it any rougher on you."

"So you wound up walking away from me altogether?"

"I didn't walk away, Patty."

"What else would you call it?"

"I'm not calling it anything."

"And you're not calling *me*, either!"

"Patty, I don't want to trade fast remarks with you. I just want you to quit that job!"

"Are you asking me or telling me?"

"Hey," he said, "this isn't getting us anywhere. But if you want an answer, this is an ultimatum. I cannot take the teasing anymore, especially when *I'm* doing what *you* should be doing."

Patty sat there, momentarily stunned. "What does that mean?"

"Nothing. Forget I said that. You'd just have to be there, that's all, to understand what's been going on."

"Hey, Kevin, I heard those same kinds of remarks. The guys at the site put me through some terrible things, and it took a lot out of me to deal with it. But now I've gotten to the point where I'm accepted as one of the crew. Kevin, I've earned something all by myself that I'm really proud of—the respect of people who didn't believe I'd amount to anything. Can you understand why that means so much to me?"

Kevin met Patty's explanation with stony silence.

"Say something, Kevin."

"There's nothing to say."

"Since when does what other people think mean more than what we feel for each other? I can't believe that you would let what they say come between us. You wouldn't let that happen. There must be something—or someone—else."

"There's nothing else! I told you my real reason, and you just don't want to make the choice," Kevin said, anger and hurt in his voice.

"It's not fair to ask me to give up something I love doing. If only I make you understand how much this job means to me."

"Patty, I told you how I feel." By the way he said it, Patty knew Kevin's mind was made up. "Now it's your decision. What happens from this point on is up to you." With that, he turned on his heel and walked back up the stairs, leaving Patty alone in the living room.

Chapter Ten

If Patty had found it unbearable not knowing why Kevin had been avoiding her, it was even worse knowing just what was wrong. What made her position so difficult was that she now knew how she could get him back—and she just couldn't do it. She felt terrible about all the teasing he'd had to put up with. But at the same time she knew he was wrong to want her to give up her work. If people were going to be insensitive and stupid about her job, she saw no reason to cater to them.

Kevin wanted Patty to give up either her work or him. And she didn't want to do either. So she ended up not making any choice at all.

She went to work every day, and she still thought almost constantly about Kevin.

Still, Patty knew that avoiding the problem wouldn't work for long. This became very clear to her one evening when she went with Steve to the movies and to an ice-cream shop afterward. Chatting happily, she grabbed the first available booth, discovering too late that Kevin and a girl she didn't recognize were sharing a booth right across from them. What made it even worse was that they were double-dating with Billy and Erica, something Kevin had always done with her. Suddenly Patty had a sickening thought. What if he had waited long enough for her answer and had made the decision for her? She was heartsick with worry. She couldn't choose to lose him, but now it might be too late! She was going to have to come to terms with this whole thing, and soon.

That Saturday afternoon, to cheer herself up after a morning of thinking about her still unresolved problem, Patty went into Mountain Fashion to browse for some new school clothes. She searched carefully through the racks of tank tops, cotton shorts, fall sweaters, and wool skirts. *What a mixed-up time*

August is, she thought. *The stores don't know whether to convince you that it's still summer and there's a lot of hot weather yet to come, or that winter is fast approaching and it's time to start buying leg warmers.* Feeling that her life was confused without another decision to have to make, she grabbed several wash-and-wear blouses appropriate for any season and headed for the dressing rooms. Yanking open one of the three curtains at the rear of the store, she immediately pulled it back into place and gasped. In the dressing room, halfway into a pair of Calvin Klein jeans, stood Gail.

"Don't you dare!" cried the voice from inside the fitting room. Patty turned back just in time to see the curtain yanked back open again.

"Here I've been scheming for days, trying to engineer a close encounter of the accidental kind, and you're running out on me." Although Gail's words were lighthearted, Patty could read in her eyes the same uncertainty she herself was feeling.

"Well, uh, I was just going to try these things on. . . ." Nervously Patty took a step toward the next dressing room.

"Hold it. Can't you stand still long enough

for me to get into these jeans and come out and apologize?"

Caught by surprise, Patty turned and waited. As she stood there, a gentle ache began to stir in her heart, a reminder of how very much she had missed her friend.

The curtain opened, and Gail came out. "How about I buy you a soda somewhere?"

"Sounds great," Patty said softly. "I'd like that—a lot."

Soon the two of them were comfortably seated in a booth at the luncheonette. They began their heart to heart over milkshakes. This time, there were no I-told-you-so's when Gail listened to what Patty was telling her.

"What I want to know, Patty, is why, after this break-up with Kevin—"

"It's not definitely over yet, Gail. At least, I don't think it is. There still might be a chance to save it."

"I want to talk more about that in a minute. But, why are you still working yourself to the bone and tying up your entire summer with this job? After all, I seem to remember that the only reason you wanted to get a job in the first place was to make enough money for Kevin's birthday present."

"That's true," Patty admitted.

"So now, you may lose Kevin over a job that was supposed to be a way of doing something wonderful for him. It doesn't make sense."

"It doesn't—but it does. Let me see if I can explain this to you. Somewhere along the line my reasons for working got all switched around. Maybe it was because I was challenged from day one to be better than I thought I could be. Maybe I discovered something in myself I didn't know was there before. I don't know. But at some point, the money just wasn't that important anymore. Does that make any sense to you?"

"It's beginning to. Go on."

"I don't know. I just couldn't let my job go. I guess maybe I knew I wouldn't like myself much if I quit. It would be like giving up."

"You know, Patty, I owe you a big apology," Gail said. "I didn't realize what you were going through, what you were learning. I just looked at the situation from the outside, without trying to really understand."

"Gail, I have to apologize for never trying to explain to you and never calling you after that awful day. I mean, if you hadn't dragged me over here, we might never have talked at all."

"Well, if you hadn't caught me off guard today, I don't know if I'd ever have gotten the nerve to call you. But I'm sure glad it worked out this way."

"I am, too," Patty said, reaching out to grab her friend's hand.

She looked happily at Gail. It felt good to have one of the problems in her life worked out. But she still had one giant problem. And Patty had no idea how she was going to find a solution.

Chapter Eleven

That Friday, as they were knocking off work, Steve mysteriously called Patty aside. "I thought I'd better tell you first, before the word got around to the rest of the guys, because you mean something special to me."

"You're a special friend to me, too, Steve. What's up?"

"Well, today is my last day working here."

"You're kidding? What happened?"

Steve sighed sadly. "My grandmother died suddenly yesterday."

"I'm sorry," Patty said gently.

"Well, she was pretty old. It's still very hard to accept. She was really great, so funny and active and kind. She'd never really been sick, so it caught us all by surprise. She lives—lived—in Maryland. She had a big old farmhouse there. I used to spend the summers with her when I was a kid. Anyway, it needs a lot of fixing up before we sell it, so I'm going down there to do repairs for the rest of the summer. It's strange. My father and I offered so many times to go down and work on the house, but either he or I or my grandmother was always too busy. So now it gets done when my heart's not in it."

Patty touched Steve's arm softly. "I can tell you loved her a lot."

"I did. I still do. You know, she once told me that if I keep her in my memory, she'll always be close to me. . . ." His voice trailed off.

"I'm going to miss you, Steve. You've been a good friend to me when I've really needed one. You've helped me through more than one rough day. And you've taught me a lot about building."

"Well, I'll be back the middle of September, so I hope I'll be seeing more of you then."

"I hope so, too."

"And I hope you can patch things up with that guy. Patty, he's crazy for not hanging onto a good person like you."

Patty smiled. So Steve had known all along. "There aren't a whole lot of people who would have understood and hung in with me like you did."

Steve smiled shyly, then looked away, a little embarrassed, and changed the subject. "I didn't want to leave on such short notice. But Mike is being really great about it. He told me not to worry and that he'd find a replacement by Monday." He laughed. "Of course, now that I think of it, it doesn't feel too great to be told just how easily I can be replaced."

"You're one friend," Patty said, "that *I* can't so easily replace."

"Hey!" He pretended to sock her under the chin. "You knock me out, you know that? Well, I guess I'd better be off. Now you take care of yourself. And I hope everything works out for you—if you know what I mean."

Patty gave him a quick sisterly hug. "You too, Steve."

Patty's weekend was definitely looking better than the past few weeks had. Phone calls were beginning to trickle in once again. Besides hearing from Gail, Patty got three other calls, a definite improvement from her previous average of zero. It seemed that finally people were managing to come to terms with what she did to earn money. Everyone, that is, except Kevin. Each time the phone rang, Patty held her breath, hoping against hope that it would be Kevin on the other end. But she waited in vain.

Nonetheless, she went to work Monday morning, feeling better than she had in weeks. Mike put her on a new project that morning. A six-foot skylight was being installed in the bathroom ceiling, and Patty was going to seal the area against leaks with roofing tar.

"Be careful with that stuff," Tom had called out to her as she made her way up the ladder, trowel and can of tar in hand.

"Don't worry," she had joked. "I've already had breakfast, I won't eat it."

Inching her way up the sloping roof, Patty stopped just under the skylight opening and braced herself to keep from slipping. Next, she opened the tar can and dipped in the trowel. She noticed that a glob of black ooze had gotten stuck on the inside of her wrist, and reached for the cleaning rag in her left pocket. She wiped the tar away and picked up the trowel once more. But now, to her disgust, Patty discovered that her whole arm was covered in the sticky stuff. The rag had rubbed against the tar somewhere. Instead of wiping the tar away, she had pressed down on the cloth with more force to get the stuff off her. A squishy, gooey sensation cooled her kneecaps. She could feel it right through her jeans.

"Ughhh!" So that was what Tom's warning was about. It was as if the tar had a life of its own, almost as if it had magical powers to pop onto anything that came within three feet of it. Patty sat back down, not caring any longer how full of tar she got. Her nose itched, and before she could stop herself, she had scratched it. She sat back and laughed. She could imagine what a mess she must look like.

After that, having made her peace with the tar, Patty settled back to work. Trying to make up for lost time, she paid little attention to the group of men gathering below. They must be meeting the new assistant, Patty thought, turning back to what she was doing. She hoped that they were not planning the same reception for this new person that she herself had been given. Patty decided then that she would make herself a friendly face to the newcomer on the site. She wondered vaguely if the new man would be someone to whom she would have to prove herself all over again. Well, even so, she knew she could handle it. She went on with her work for another fifteen minutes until she scraped the sides of the near-empty tar can. Another lay at the bottom of the ladder.

Walking down the ladder, she was startled to feel someone poke her gently on the arm. She whirled around and got the shock of her life.

It was Kevin.

"Wha—what are you doing here?"

"I work here."

"You work here? What do you mean?" she asked, bewildered. Then the realization hit her. "You're the new assistant?"

"You got it!" Kevin grinned.

"I don't understand."

"Well, I'd like to explain it to you. Can I do it over a pizza after work?"

The question brought up mixed feelings. On the one hand, Patty was curious—very curious—to find out about this sudden reappearance of Kevin. But on the other hand, there was a feeling of being closed in!

What right does he have to show up suddenly like this? Patty asked herself. *Just when I was beginning to feel more in control of my life. He's ignored me, he's avoided me,*

*and suddenly he pops up behind me. I just
don't need it!*

What amazed her was—in spite of all
these thoughts—to hear herself answering,
"All right."

Kevin beamed. "We'll go right after
work."

"No!" replied Patty, reasserting her control over the situation. "I'll meet you there."
She wanted to go home and wash up and
change first, but she didn't tell him that.
There was no need to explain herself.

Kevin had seemed so casual and self-
confident when he had first approached Patty
on the ladder. But all of that was shattered
now, and it was plain to Patty that Kevin's
calm appearance had just been an act.

"Uh—yeah—sure. Uh, what time is good
for you? Is—six-thirty OK? Or—uh—would
you like to make it later?"

"Six-thirty would be fine." Patty smiled.

"Can't I pick you up at your house?"

"All right. But I have to get back to work
now."

"Oh, sure thing." Kevin said as she clam-
bered up the rungs of the ladder.

After her shower Patty glanced into the

bathroom mirror and studied herself for a moment. *What should I wear?* she asked herself. Wrapping a towel around her wet hair, Patty left the bathroom and headed straight for her clothes closet. She flipped through the hangers and instinctively selected a marvelously shimmery black- and red-striped blouse. If anything was going to knock Kevin out, it would be this top with her black cotton pants. But as she lay the outfit out on her bed, Patty suddenly caught herself.

What am I doing? she thought. *Why do I want to knock Kevin out? Why am I trying to hard to make a good impression after the way he's treated me?*

Patty's mood swung abruptly in a completely different direction. *What do I care what he thinks about the way I look?* she thought bitterly. She began to feel her resentment rising, remembering the growing humiliation she had felt during those lonely nights of waiting for the phone calls that never came. She felt once more the sense of betrayal that had come over her when she had seen Kevin at the lake with that other girl. Worst of all had been the discovery that he wasn't going to stand by her when she needed him.

Why am I going out with him at all? she asked herself. *So now he's decided it's time to forgive and forget because—I don't even know why. And I'm supposed to be thrilled that he's come back to me.* A new thought occurred to her. *I don't even know that for certain. Maybe he's going to tell me that he's fallen in love with somebody else.* She felt a sudden stab of fear.

This is all craziness! she told herself. *I'm just going to go and find out what he has to tell me. And I'll wear what makes me feel good.*

"Hey, you look great!" Kevin said as Patty emerged from her house. She had decided on a neat pair of jeans and a green cotton sweater.

"Thank you."

As they drove down her street, Kevin remarked, "It looks like the trees have really recovered from the gypsy moths, haven't they?"

"Yes," Patty answered politely. "They're very pretty."

"Hey, did you hear that Coach Watson was arrested for drunk driving?"

"Kevin," Patty said softly, "I really don't want to make small talk. I think you asked me out to discuss something, so why don't we just start talking?"

Kevin let out a deep sigh and carefully pulled the car over to the side of the road. The thought that he might reach over to kiss her made Patty feel uncomfortable. She didn't know how she would respond. But Kevin didn't make any movement toward her at all. In fact, he kept his eyes turned toward the road, as if still driving.

"I—uh—want to apologize. But I'm not sure how to. . . ." His voice trailed off.

Patty contained a sigh of relief. "I don't know, either. I guess you should just begin."

"OK. Well, I really do want to tell you how bad I feel about everything that has happened. And especially about my giving you an ultimatum about quitting and all that stuff. And, also, I want to tell you that I was pretty— pretty jealous when I saw you with that good-looking guy at the lake. I mean, you really looked like you were happy with him. Like you two were a couple or something. That got to me."

For the first time, Kevin turned to look at Patty. "Is there something between you two?"

"Considering that you haven't called me in such a long time and that you've probably been out with a lot of people—including that girl I saw *you* with at the beach, I really don't see why I have to answer that."

"Well—well," Kevin stammered, "I—I'm just trying to find out where things stand between us."

"I don't know myself, Kevin," Patty answered sincerely.

Suddenly Kevin leaned toward her, taking her hands in his. "Patty—" he began.

She felt the pressure of his fingers upon her palms, but she couldn't—or wouldn't—bring herself to respond. Hesitantly Kevin withdrew his hands.

"I guess it *is* all over," he said darkly.

"I didn't say that."

For a long while they sat in silence, lost in their own thoughts.

Kevin began at last. "These last few weeks have been torture for me."

"It wasn't always so great for me, either."

"Yeah, I know. Boy!" he exclaimed with a little laugh. "This is a lot harder than I thought it was going to be."

"Do you want to end it, Kevin, and take me home?"

"What about the pizza?"

"I can live without the pizza."

A hurt expression came over Kevin's face. "Why did you come out with me at all?"

"I—wanted to hear why you took the job."

"Why? Because I really wanted it from the beginning."

"I don't get it," Patty said almost defensively. "You're the one who told me about it in the first place. Why didn't you go after it yourself if you really wanted it?"

"I guess I was scared. You know, it was easy for me to work another summer at the Grand Union. There was no problem applying, the manager liked me, and I got along well with the other workers. I just didn't want to—well—go for the job and—and not get it! I would have thought that I was only good enough to work at a checkout counter." He gave a self-mocking laugh.

"But that's ridiculous, Kevin."

"Yeah, well, I know that it is, but still . . ." His voice trailed off.

"You mean," Patty said, "that it wasn't all the teasing about me that got you down, but because I took the job you were afraid to apply for?"

"The teasing was part of it. But I could have lived with the teasing.

"The night you came over to the house, when you said that there had to be another

131

reason for my acting like that to you, I wasn't going to admit anything to myself then, but after you left, I started to think. And I guess it's really because I love you so much that I finally had to be honest with myself. Because, Patty—I really was covering up. I mean, I felt you were taking the job that I'd have applied for myself if I wasn't such a coward about it. And that's why I applied for the job this time, when I found out there was another opening. Look," Kevin said smiling softly. "I was lucky enough to get a second chance at the job. Do you think, maybe—that I can get a second chance with you?"

Patty sighed. "Well, Kevin—you know—this thing hurt me pretty badly. And I'm not sure *how* I feel right now. I just think I need some time. . . ."

Patty's words faded away into a silence that lasted for a few minutes. Finally Kevin spoke. "Yeah, I can understand that. Do you want me to take you home now?"

The sadness in his eyes touched her. "Kevin—" Patty put out her hand and placed it lightly on his shoulder. "Did I say I wasn't sure about being hungry?"

"No!" Kevin brightened. "You didn't." A grin spread over his face as he added, "There have been so many changes around here lately, that I think I'd better ask—are you still big on mushroom and pepper pizzas?"

"They're still my favorite!"

"So are you," Kevin said softly.

"I'm glad to hear that."

"Are you really?"

Patty let her smile give the answer.

"Well, then, what are we waiting for?" Kevin exclaimed, turning the key in the ignition.

As the car spun off toward town, Patty thought over the events of the last several weeks. She remembered how hard it had been on that first day at the construction site, even just to walk past all the staring men. And then came the practical jokes aimed at forcing her to give up and quit. But now, she knew, the crew really accepted her as one of them. All by herself, she had earned their respect.

Patty's thoughts turned back to Kevin, sitting beside her at the wheel. Perhaps now she faced the most difficult hurdle of all.

What's going to happen to us? she wondered. *Will I ever be able to trust him again, the way I did before?*

Patty didn't know the answer to that. Not yet. So many things had happened in those few short weeks. But she did know that she had changed. She felt stronger, more confident, more independent.

And suddenly Patty realized that, one way or another, everything was going to work out just fine.

You'll fall in love with all the Sweet Dream romances.
Reading these stories, you'll be reminded of yourself or of
someone you know. There's Jennie, the *California Girl*,
who becomes an outsider when her family moves to Texas.
And Cindy, the *Little Sister*, who's afraid that Christine,
the oldest in the family, will steal her new boyfriend.
Don't miss any of the Sweet Dreams romances.

☐	24292	**IT MUST BE MAGIC #26** Marian Woodruff	**$2.25**
☐	22681	**TOO YOUNG FOR LOVE #27** Gailanne Maravel	**$1.95**
☐	23053	**TRUSTING HEARTS #28** Jocelyn Saal	**$1.95**
☐	24312	**NEVER LOVE A COWBOY #29** Jesse Dukore	**$2.25**
☐	24293	**LITTLE WHITE LIES #30** Lois I. Fisher	**$2.25**
☐	23189	**TOO CLOSE FOR COMFORT #31** Debra Spector	**$1.95**
☐	24837	**DAY DREAMER #32** Janet Quin-Harkin	**$2.25**
☐	23283	**DEAR AMANDA #33** Rosemary Vernon	**$1.95**
☐	23287	**COUNTRY GIRL #34** Melinda Pollowitz	**$1.95**
☐	24336	**FORBIDDEN LOVE #35** Marian Woodruff	**$2.25**
☐	24338	**SUMMER DREAMS #36** Barbara Conklin	**$2.25**
☐	23340	**PORTRAIT OF LOVE #37** Jeanette Noble	**$1.95**
☐	24331	**RUNNING MATES #38** Jocelyn Saal	**$2.25**
☐	24340	**FIRST LOVE #39** Debra Spector	**$2.25**
☐	24315	**SECRETS #40** Anna Aaron	**$2.25**
☐	24838	**THE TRUTH ABOUT ME AND BOBBY V. #41** Janetta Johns	**$2.25**
☐	23532	**THE PERFECT MATCH #42** Marian Woodruff	**$1.95**
☐	23533	**TENDER-LOVING-CARE #43** Anne Park	**$1.95**
☐	23534	**LONG DISTANCE LOVE #44** Jesse Dukore	**$1.95**
☐	24341	**DREAM PROM #45** Margaret Burman	**$2.25**
☐	23697	**ON THIN ICE #46** Jocelyn Saal	**$1.95**
☐	23743	**TE AMO MEANS I LOVE YOU #47** Deborah Kent	**$1.95**
☐	24688	**SECRET ADMIRER #81** Debra Spector	**$2.25**
☐	24383	**HEY, GOOD LOOKING #82** Jane Polcovar	**$2.25**

Prices and availability subject to change without notice.

☐	25033	**DOUBLE LOVE #1**	$2.50
☐	25044	**SECRETS #2**	$2.50
☐	25034	**PLAYING WITH FIRE #3**	$2.50
☐	25143	**POWER PLAY #4**	$2.50
☐	25043	**ALL NIGHT LONG #5**	$2.50
☐	25105	**DANGEROUS LOVE #6**	$2.50
☐	25106	**DEAR SISTER #7**	$2.50
☐	25092	**HEARTBREAKER #8**	$2.50
☐	25026	**RACING HEARTS #9**	$2.50
☐	25016	**WRONG KIND OF GIRL #10**	$2.50
☐	25046	**TOO GOOD TO BE TRUE #11**	$2.50
☐	25035	**WHEN LOVE DIES #12**	$2.50
☐	24524	**KIDNAPPED #13**	$2.25
☐	24531	**DECEPTIONS #14**	$2.50
☐	24582	**PROMISES #15**	$2.50
☐	24672	**RAGS TO RICHES #16**	$2.50
☐	24723	**LOVE LETTERS #17**	$2.50

Prices and availability subject to change without notice.

Buy them at your local bookstore or use this handy coupon for ordering:

Bantam Books, Inc., Dept SVH, 414 East Golf Road, Des Plaines, Ill. 60016

Please send me the books I have checked above. I am enclosing $_____
(please add $1.25 to cover postage and handling). Send check or money order
—no cash or C.O.D.'s please.

Mr/Mrs/Miss _____

Address_____

City_____ State/Zip_____

SVH—3/85

Please allow four to six weeks for delivery. This offer expires 9/85.

SPECIAL
MONEY SAVING
OFFER

Now you can have an up-to-date listing of Bantam's hundreds of titles plus take advantage of our unique and exciting bonus book offer. A special offer which gives you the opportunity to purchase a Bantam book for only 50¢. Here's how!

By ordering any five books at the regular price per order, you can also choose any other single book listed (up to a $4.95 value) for just 50¢. Some restrictions do apply, but for further details why not send for Bantam's listing of titles today!

Just send us your name and address plus 50¢ to defray the postage and handling costs.
